Just a Little Crush

Holly June Smith

Cover design by Frankie Rose Illustration

For filthbags everywhere

Contents

1

Bec

Why does he have to look like that?

I spot him through the shop window when he pauses to help Mrs Fairbanks cross the street safely. She's such a scam artist, but it seems the women of our little town are not short of ways to get their hands on Alistair Rendall. I can't say I blame them.

There he goes, in dark grey cargo trousers, the sleeves of his white t-shirt straining around his enormous arms, black hoodie slung casually over his shoulder. Even when he's not in uniform, he's got his own personal one.

His dark hair is pushed back from his face, the way he always styles it when he showers quickly after his shift. It's getting a little long, he must be due to have it cut this week or next. He could be a model with that strong jaw and those piercing eyes and that neck.

My god.

The things I would do to that neck.

He stoops to give Mrs Fairbanks a peck on the cheek, flashing a bright smile as he sends her on her way and stalks a path towards my door. Those full lips. Those perfect teeth. He runs a hand through his hair and everything inside me clenches. *Goddammit, is he moving in slow-motion?*

Thankfully, it's brighter outside than in here so I know he can't see me ogling him for the bajillionth time. He won't have a clue that I'm tracking my eyes over his biceps and wondering what they would feel like to grip onto from underneath him. He won't see me counting the abs that his tight t-shirt does nothing to hide, or dreaming about what that unmissable bulge in his trousers conceals. And he won't see me rolling my eyes when one of the tennis mums intercepts him to flip her hair and laugh and flirt.

I don't know why they bother. Alistair Rendall doesn't date. Haven't they figured it out by now? He's a wife guy, and someday soon the perfect woman will walk into his life. She'll be a saint, a schoolteacher or something, and for years people will say she was the most beautiful bride this town has ever seen. She'll make him a perfect home and give gentle birth to three blond cherubs. She'll bake cakes for the station fundraiser, host a book club where they'll describe the books as feminist masterpieces, and she'll have a cold beer and a hot dinner ready for him when he gets home from work. Hell, she'll probably even get asked to turn on the town lights at Christmas.

Alas, this woman on the street is not the wife he's after, and I watch him politely decline whatever it is she's trying to pitch to him.

He's always been just Rennie to me. It's a nickname from school that stuck around, along with his good guy reputation. Rennie is, in fact, the most gentlemanly gentleman you'll ever meet, except in my dirty mind where he's *quite* the opposite. It's a damn shame. A cruel trick. A waste of a hot, ripped body to put such a decent man inside it.

I've spent years wondering what he would be like if he wasn't so bloody nice. Would he barge in here, round the counter, push me into the back of the shop and ravage me up against the refrigerator unit? I wish he would.

The shop bell rings when he pushes the door open. I snap out of my fantasy and try to act as if I'm surprised by his arrival. Though I will secretly admit that seeing Rennie is the best part of my week, because it means I get to concoct a fresh new sexy scenario.

"Morning, Bec," he says. Ugh, there's that smile again. His smile makes you feel like the only person in the room. He always smells so good, a faint mix of smoke and something clean and herbal. I can smell it even over the stinkiest cheeses I have on sale. "What have you got for me today?"

"Oh, hey, Rennie." *Act casual, act casual.* I wipe my sweaty palms on my apron. "It's goat's cheese, honey, and rocket today."

"With the rosemary walnut bread?" he asks.

"That's the one."

The sound that comes out of his mouth is so sexual it sends my insides into a spin. "You know those are my favourite. I'll take two."

I try not to think about how much I want him to make that noise between my legs and immediately fail.

"You say that about every sandwich I make," I let out a laugh like a besotted teenager, and stop it instantly. "You want me to warm them up for you?"

"Yes, please." He opens the drinks fridge near the door, pausing to cool down in front of it for a few seconds, just like always. It's one of my favourite things to witness because I know it means he's hot, and the idea that he would be scorching to touch excites me like nothing else. I transfer his lunch to the sandwich press and ring up his order.

Serving specialty cheese toasties was Rennie's idea in the first place, and it's been great for business. Every morning my friend Sarah brings fresh loaves from her bakery, The Floury Godmother, and I get to work making sandwiches before the lunch rush.

I inherited my cheesemonger business from my Grandpa five years ago. I've been working here since I was sixteen though, unofficially, Gramps put me to work as soon as I could hand customers their cheese without demanding they give it back. I know that kind of thing might have a lot of people feeling stuck, but this shop is my life. When Gramps died, I knew I'd never go anywhere else. He'd had a good run at it, still working into his late 80s. By the time he left us, my dad was retired and ready to spend his days hauling my mum around Europe in their new campervan. It was my turn to step up, and I was proud to do it.

Though business was doing OK back then, I knew it could do even better. I'd already convinced Gramps to launch a wedding catering service, which I was running single-handedly. Now I have an assistant manager, Alyssa, who helps me with that side of things so I can stay on top of the rest.

I've given the store a bit of a makeover too. Though the main counter has been replaced with a more modern refrigeration unit, I've kept the walls the original dark green they've always been. It matches our staff aprons and reminds me of him. We still have our original cash register, though on the counter behind it you'll also find an iPad and card reader, since the majority of our customers don't use much cash these days.

Along one side of the shop Rennie helped me build shelving out of old wooden crates and I stocked them with more crackers, chutneys, pickles, and sauces than one person could eat in a lifetime. At the back of the store we have a selection of English wines and craft beers, and I host intimate cheese and wine nights that always sell out.

At Christmas I have to hire a team of ten, mostly kids back home from university for the holidays. It's chaos, but the shop becomes a non-stop party, and everyone loves it. We play carols, keep a vat of mulled wine topped up, and last year I even got a write up in The Sunday Times as one of the top ten cheesemongers in the UK. So yes, business is good, I love it here, and I don't think I could make my Gramps more proud.

Rennie brings his drink and a bag of salt and vinegar crisps to the counter, and takes out his wallet. He's had the same one for years, the brown leather all soft and worn but reliable as ever.

I hold out the card reader for him and I'm grateful it takes a while to connect because it gives me longer to stare at his hands. Those beautiful long fingers, the underside of his wrists I dream of licking because I am an insane woman with an out-of-control libido.

"How are the kids today?" I ask. Not content with being a super-hero firefighter, Rennie also spends his spare time teaching self-de-fence classes, and volunteering to host Rhyme Time at our local li-brary. It used to be run by the librarians, but it was so poorly attended that they decided to cancel it.

I can't *possibly* imagine why Renn taking over turned things around. On Wednesdays, every toddler in a thirty-mile radius is dragged along to sit on the floor and listen to him while their mums bat their eye-lashes and twirl their hair.

I shouldn't complain, it's great for local businesses and who am I to judge other women for having a little crush? Lord knows I've been horny for this man since the day I hit puberty.

"They are as precious as ever, although I think Amanda's kid has eaten way too much broccoli this week." His nose wrinkles at some rancid memory. "And Stacey's boy needs to learn a thing or two about personal space. She kept having to rescue him from my lap while I read *'Guess How Much I Love You?'*"

"Oh, I bet she was so disappointed about that," I smile and raise an eyebrow. He knows all the women around here will use any excuse to hit on him.

The sizzle of the hot grill calls me back to his sandwiches, and I carefully lift them with tongs and slide them into their waxed paper bag.

"You got a wedding this weekend?" he asks.

"Two. One up at Fenwick's and one in a family garden."

"A garden wedding with this forecast? I hope that marquee is extra secure. I don't want to get a call about anything taking flight."

"I know. Hopefully the only person getting blown is the groom."

Oh god, why am I like this? I force a laugh but groan inwardly when he just stares at me blankly. I pick up a cloth to wipe the counter clear of crumbs that don't exist, desperate for something to look at that isn't him. He clears his throat to break the awkward silence.

"Well, good luck with it all," he says, heading for the door. "See you when I see you."

All I can do is watch that perfect, juicy, squeezable, biteable ass walk away from me and wish I could reach out and touch it. When he turns without warning, I forget he's actually in the room with me, and take far too long to look back up to his eyeline.

"Hey Bec, are you dating anyone right now?" *Me? Dating? Why is he asking?* I don't date. I wouldn't be able to show my face in this town if I went out with someone, got to know them, told them what I was into, and got dumped. Again.

"No, why?"

"We have a new guy who just joined the station. Our age, single. You looking to get set up?"

Perfect. Another nice guy with a nice job in a nice town. If I wanted a nice guy I'd probably be married by now, but I don't want a nice guy. I want a bad guy, a rough guy, a guy who'll give me what I need before I even know I need it. I want Rennie. Hard, naked, pinning me to the mattress while he—

"Bec?"

Shit. Fantasising, again. "That's OK, I don't need to be set up. Send him to see the tennis mums."

He laughs with his whole, broad chest. "OK. Well, I'm sure you'll meet him eventually. You take care."

I wait for him to disappear from my view before flipping over the 'Back in 5 Minutes' sign and locking the door. Rushing through the Staff Only door at the rear of the shop, I take the stairs two at a time, up to the little flat I call home.

As if 5 minutes with my vibrator will ever be enough to get my mind out of the gutter, or this guy out of my mind.

2

Rennie

A blow job joke? Is she seriously cracking blow job jokes in front of me like I'm not going to be affected by that? I couldn't think of anything else the entire walk home, which thankfully wasn't far, despite taking the longer route along the lane by the riverbank. I'm keeping an eye on a wall I've noticed is crumbling away. I submitted a report to the council weeks ago, but I know the maintenance department is a man down and stretched. Once this stormy weather passes, I reckon I'll just sort it myself.

I'm pretty relieved Bec said she's not looking to get set up. When Leon joined our crew and mentioned he was hoping to meet someone, it didn't take long for her name to come up. It took every ounce of restraint not to shout "No, mine," but she's not mine, and she never will be.

I asked her if she was dating so she'd have fair warning if he does approach her, though my motives were hardly innocent. I never see her with anyone, but that doesn't mean I know every detail of her private life. For all I know, she could have some guy in the city, or a long distance thing on the go.

In truth, I asked because I want to know for myself, and thank fuck I got the answer I was looking for. At least now she's prepped to say no when Leon asks her out, rather than having something sprung on her.

And he will ask, because you'd have to be out of your mind not to want to try to get her out on a date.

Bec's name comes up in far more conversations than I'd like. Thatch Cross is the kind of town where someone mentions your name before you've opened your eyes and set your feet on the ground. If you're lucky, folks are singing your praises. If you're not so lucky, they're speculating on your business, and if you're me and Bec, they're usually trying to set you up. Though, of course, never with each other. Nobody sees us like that.

It's been that way since Sophie left. From the second she got on that plane, there was a sort of collective mourning period. For weeks I couldn't go into a shop, pub, or cafe without someone cornering me to tell me how sorry they were. How much they'd miss her. I suppose I was lucky that she told everyone she wanted to travel, even if it was only half of the truth. If they knew the rest of it, it wouldn't be words of sympathy they'd have for me.

After I plate up my lunch, I take it to the dining table with this bullshit can of fancy citrus water I grabbed from Bec's fridge without looking. Half the first sandwich is gone in one bite. When the warm honey and sharp cheese hits my tongue, I groan out loud. Bec's toasties are the highlight of my week. Yes, because they're delicious, but also because it buys me a few minutes of her time I've no other excuse to get.

I'm not really one for socialising. Sometimes I'll have a few beers after work, or I'll get invited to a family dinner with one of the crew, though I've stopped accepting invites after being tricked into a few double dates that I would never have said yes to.

Work keeps me busy, and the gym, volunteering, and keeping my parents' house in order.

I grew up in a house across the road from Bec's parents, but when my folks retired a few years ago, they downsized to this bungalow. Said it was somewhere they could live out the rest of their days. About five minutes later they realised they were bored, so they bought a holiday apartment in Spain, and are currently driving somewhere in Europe with Bec's Mum and Dad in a campervan.

It didn't make sense for me to keep living in my flat while their house sat empty, so the place is pretty much mine. There's a decent kitchen and lounge area, three good-sized bedrooms, and a south facing patio that's the perfect spot for a beer after a long day. Or a bowl of cereal if I'm just home from a night shift.

The only thing missing is someone to spend it with.

It's not that I'm lonely. I have plenty of friends and a great team at work who are more like brothers and sisters than colleagues, but I do sometimes wish I could come home to someone. Someone with a sense of humour, who I could talk to for hours. Someone with a soft, warm body that would fit perfectly against mine. Someone who's into the stuff I'm into. Someone like Bec.

Except Bec isn't like me. She's a fucking sweetheart. If you cut her open, I'm pretty sure her chest would be filled with candy hearts and gummy bears. She's got that happy, busy energy that you just want to be around, and she knows everything about everyone and everything that has ever happened in this town. Not because she's a gossip, but because people genuinely want her in their lives. Last year two people gave their babies the middle name Rebecca after her. I'm not even joking.

Yet her sweetness is a curse because she's also got the hottest body I've ever seen, all soft and curvy, just how I like it. She's gorgeous even in her green shop apron. She wears these vest tops and denim shorts through summer that make her arse look like a peach. They drive me wild, but I don't even feel sad when she swaps them for the Carhartt work trousers she wears all winter because they look just as good. But that apron...

Fuck, I've probably imagined her wearing that and nothing else every day of my adult life. I'm jealous of any man who ever gets to see her naked because I know I never will.

She has this cute button nose, gorgeous pink lips, and she always gets a sprinkle of freckles across her cheeks when she's been out in the sun for too long. She wears her long, dark hair piled up on top of her head and every time I see her I want to shove my hands in it and pull her mouth to mine.

I'm not the only one. I don't know how many guys have tried to ask her out over the years but, bar one guy who she dated after school, she's always stayed single. Sometimes I hear guys talking about her around town, but a firm word usually shuts them right up.

I'm a bastard for doing it though, because it's not like I would ever dare make a move on Bec. She's far too good for the likes of me, but I'm still protective of her. Maybe a little too protective at times, but we've grown up together, it's understandable. Our parents are friends, our grandparents were friends, and we're the only two from our school year who've stuck around.

We had a decent group of friends here in our teens. Some travelled to the other side of the world and stayed put, a few moved away and only come back for Christmas.

It's not like this place is dying though. There's been a steady influx of new folks looking to swap the city life for a country one, and plenty of friendly faces amongst them.

But the one constant is Bec, and it wouldn't be the place it is without her. She gives her life to this town. She organises so many events throughout the year, all the street decorations at Christmas. She sends care packages when people are unwell, checks in on her Grandpa's friends, and goes to their 90th birthday parties because she genuinely wants to, not just because she's known them her whole life.

She's smart too. She was running the show long before her Gramps officially handed the shop over to her. She's full of ideas, one of those people who loves bringing people together. She's perfect.

And apparently she makes blow job jokes, and it's all I can think about.

Bec on her knees.

Bec with her tongue out.

Bec sucking me down deep.

Bec whimpering when I grab her hair and hold her in place.

Bec.

Bec.

Bec.

For fucks sake. I can't even make it past lunchtime, what is wrong with me? I drop my half-eaten toastie onto my plate and head down the hallway to my bedroom. Kicking the door closed behind me, my zipper is already down, and I wrap my fist around my dick. It's a pointless gesture. There's nobody to interrupt me, and still I do it because I know I shouldn't be doing this. Shouldn't be stroking my dick in the middle of the day thinking about Bec. Or any hour of the day.

She's too good for you. She's too good for you. She's too good for you.

A useless fucking mantra. All it does is spur me on. The thought of her perfect, womanly body, laid out on my bed waiting for me to make my move. To act out every depraved fantasy I've ever had about her. If I had one chance with her, I'd take all goddamn night. I'd pin her down and ravage her, have her screaming that it's too much, then begging me for more. The thought of it makes me grip harder and before long I'm grunting, spilling over my hand while shame washes over me.

Yeah, damn straight she's too good for me. She's an angel who deserves the very best. And that is why a monster like me can never, ever, ever make a move on Bec.

3

Bec

The road up through the grounds of the Fenwick Estate is one of the most beautiful places you could ever drive. Vast meadows spread out on either side of the tree-lined avenue, full of the most stunning wildflowers. I always feel as if I'm in Downton Abbey or something when I take the meandering route up to the main house.

Sometimes I see deer grazing, or the ears of a hare peeking out above the long grass. Beyond the meadows lie thick oak forests that keep the house and grounds well hidden from the B-road that leads you here. If you didn't know it existed, you'd never be any the wiser, and I love that it feels like a hidden gem.

The house itself was built in the early 1800s, on the site of the previous house, which was apparently more than 700 years old. During the week, the gardens and the house are open to the public, but at weekends weddings are the order of the day, and they charge a small fortune for exclusive hire.

The couples who marry here are gorgeous, rich, and classy as hell, but in my experience as a supplier, they're often genuinely nice too. I host after hours tastings once a month, so they can sample the cheeses I recommend. In turn, they regale me with stories of how they met, their perfect proposals, their plans for the big day. The women attempt to blind me with the sparkling rocks on their fingers, and I bury any pangs of jealousy deep, deep down.

I'll probably never get married, but I'm not opposed to the idea of it. If I ever did, I'd definitely want to get married here. Mainly because I have a very specific, highly detailed fantasy that involves me being chased through the grounds of this grand house by my new husband, my dress billowing out behind me, my feet slipping in the dewy grass as I make for the woods. I'll hide, but he'll find me and catch me and I'll be railed against a tree, my bridal gown bunched up around my waist.

A girl can dream.

A wheel of sharp cheddar forms the base before I add a tall round of Colston Bassett Stilton, which surprises even the most staunch blue-cheese haters when paired with their slice of traditional wedding cake. Next is a whole wild garlic yarg, a much more vibrant green than the more common nettle version. I pause to admire the pattern the layers of leaves make, and take a close up photo to share to our Instagram. This couple have opted for a smoked cheese next, and the final layer is a heart-shaped brie, with several more spread out on the table below. It's a great choice. Give me a box of crackers and a knife, and I can take one of these beauties down in under ten minutes.

Ripe figs, plump grapes and springs of rosemary are nestled amongst each layer, enveloping the tower in an upward spiral. Next, I set up grazing boards of crackers in various shapes, flavours and sizes interspersed with jars of chutney, honey, and homemade pickles.

I stand back and view my masterpiece. No matter how many of these I make, I never get bored of imagining the guests' faces when they see it as a finished display.

I also never get bored of standing in the ballroom, imagining the thousands of couples who've danced here over the years. I picture the Elizabeths and the Darcys, the Bridgerton brood, and it wouldn't surprise me if a few of the older royals have been here at some point too. I wonder how many matches have been made, how many scandals have begun, and how many illicit snogs have been had in hidden alcoves down winding corridors. I've clocked several spots for a cheeky fumble in my time working here, and you'd best believe that I've gone straight home and imagined Rennie doing the fumbling.

When I've cleared all my supplies away, I take a few photos for our social media and give Alyssa a call to check in.

"How's it going at the Sutton's?"

"I'm just finishing up."

"The marquee still holding?" The wind has picked up in the time I've been here, and though the storm we're expecting hasn't hit yet, we're right in the path of it. That's one great benefit of a venue like this. Nobody wants to be outside when they can be in a stunning ballroom eyeing up their prince.

"Yup, the tent company had an event cancel due to the storms, so they ended up giving them a more sturdy one instead."

"Oh, fantastic. I have to admit, I didn't think it would be too bad, but it's getting wild up here."

"I mean, it's holding strong, but the wind is noisy as hell." I can hear it in the background through the phone. "As long as they love their cheese, that's all that matters to me," she says. I know they will, she's got a great eye for food styling. I'm damn lucky to have her working with me.

"I'm about to leave Fenwick's so I'll see you back at the shop. Drive safe."

"You too."

My phone buzzes just as I hang up. It's a text from Rennie telling me to be safe on the roads today. That is so like him. The busiest man in Thatch Cross, and he still finds time to look out for locals. I'm surprised he even remembers I'm up here today.

It's a thirty-minute drive back into town, and I'm in no rush. With my woodland fuck fantasy still on my mind, I load up my audio-book app, and select one I recall has a similar scene. There's no better company on my deliveries than the husky tones of a sex god book boyfriend.

That'll get me right in the mood for my quiet evening plans; a deep bath, gooey brie, a jar of pickled onions, and my freshly charged wand. Probably not all at the same time, but never say never.

Exiting the estate grounds, I turn back onto the country lane just as the rain begins to lash down. The road is already scattered with leaves and branches that definitely weren't here when I arrived, and I can feel the wind buffeting the car when I speed through open stretches. Shit, this is way sketchier than I expected, but I know my lovely little car will get me home in one piece.

As soon as the thought forms, I see a tree up ahead, jutting out at an angle not like any of the others on this stretch of road. It's too late to stop by the time I realise it's coming down.

Instinct takes over. I hit the accelerator and swerve to avoid its path, but it's hopeless. My baby spins in the road, tyres screeching, until she comes to a sudden stop in the hedgerow. I slam my eyes shut when the worst noise I've ever heard in my life fills my ears. Cracking, creaking, roaring, and crunching. The window next to me smashes into pieces all over my lap and my hands fly to my head, bracing for whatever comes next.

I don't know how long I stay like that, but when I open my eyes, I want to cry. My car. My baby. Fuck, this is bad. My head hurts. My ears are ringing. I try to sit up straight, but the roof of the car is caved in, the windscreen completely smashed by the canopy of a fallen Oak. There's glass everywhere and when I reach up to my head, I feel pieces of it caught in my bun.

Someone is shouting at me. A man, no, a woman. She's screaming, moaning, but wait... those aren't screams of pain or terror.

Oh god, oh no. It's not a person, it's my phone. Somewhere my audiobook is still playing. I try to look around for it, but my neck hurts too much to look far. It must have gotten thrown about in the crash.

I reach down blindly and manage to release my seatbelt, which gives me a little more breathing room, but shifting any further is impossible with the roof bearing down on me. My wrist twinges when I try to push open my door, and besides, it's blocked by a branch, leaves poking inside, filling whatever space they can. I try to push them out to make more space, but I scratch my arm on a conker shell, and tears spring to my eyes. This is so bad, I'm trapped. Properly trapped. My chest feels tight. I think I'm on the verge of a panic attack. I need to calm down. I need help. Where is my phone?

Think Bec, think.

OK. This could be worse. I'm OK. I'm alive. I'm not hurt, not bad, I don't think. Just sore. I will be OK. I just need to hang tight and someone will come. *Breathe Rebecca. Reframe. Turn that negative into a positive.*

I can do this. I am merely a woman having a pause during her working day, listening to her book.

Focus on the words Rebecca. Focus on those sweet, spicy words. Someone will come.

I snort at the innuendo. There is something almost funny about this. Me, trapped here, completely helpless in the company of a smutty romance. Thank god I put one on or I'd be panicking much more in silence.

I think of my shop, of Alyssa getting back and the Saturday staff wondering where I am. Will they know how to close up without me? I think of my parents, no doubt enjoying a boozy lunch in the sunshine somewhere. I think of Rennie. I've no idea what he's doing today, but I bet he looks damn good doing it.

And just like that, I'm back to imagining it's me and Rennie in this book. *Bec and Rennie up against a tree. F-U-C-K-I-N-G.*

What is wrong with me? I must be the only person on this planet who would get horny in a car accident. *Oh god. Please, someone come find me soon.*

4

Rennie

It's only a matter of time before the call we've all been expecting comes in. A tree down, blocking a country road, a car crushed underneath. The caller can't get close enough to see how many people are involved.

The location is right between us and the nearest crew, but they've been called to a warehouse fire, so we're on the road in under a minute.

We're almost there when it occurs to me that this is the back road up to the Fenwick estate. Didn't Bec say she'd booked a wedding here today? The thought is a seed that grows rapidly, roots spreading out across my stomach, vines winding up through my chest, tightening their grip until I can barely breathe.

I know it before I see it. The car. Bec's car.

I try to get out of the cab before we've even come to a stop. "Get out of my way." I barge past my crew and I'm storming towards her, jumping over fallen debris to get close. We've come from the opposite side to whoever called this in, and from here the rear driver side of her car is mostly visible, but the front is now half the height under the weight of a gigantic oak.

"Bec, Bec!" I duck under a limb of the tree and tear away at the branches and leaves covering her window until I find her slumped forward with her head in her hands.

"Bec, oh god, oh sweetheart, are you OK?" She slowly turns her gaze towards me and starts screaming.

"*Ahhh oh god oh no. Noooo.*" She starts mumbling and ranting, and I can't make out a word. Loud moans fill the car.

"Are you hurt? Stay still, just tell me where it hurts."

"Siri! Siri! Stop now. La la la la la. OK Google. Shut down. *Shut. Down. Phone. Now!*"

"Is she OK?" Leon asks over my shoulder.

"She's babbling, I think she has a concussion."

"Ambulance is on the way. Do you think she'll need to be sedated?"

"Noooo," she screams. "No needles. NO!" Fear fills her eyes, she tries to get out of the car and starts screaming again. Shit, I'd forgotten how afraid of them she is. We shouldn't have let her hear us.

I crouch beside her door and reach in to cup her face. "Bec, listen to me. You need to stop shouting and be still for a second. Just look at me, look into my eyes and breathe."

There's not a lot of space between us, most of it filled with my helmet, but when our eyes lock she stops screaming. Then I hear a man's voice.

"*I'm gonna do bad dirty things to you, you little whore.*"

It's a gruff, American, male voice. What the hell? Who is that?

"*Suck my dick like a good girl and then I'll fuck you like you want it.*"

The back of the car is pretty crushed. I can't see in properly. "Bec, is someone else in there with you?" She squeezes her eyes shut and starts groaning.

"*Oh yes, baby. Fill my tight little pussy up. I need you so bad.*"

A woman's voice now.

"*That's right. I'm gonna pump you so full of come, you'll be dripping down your thighs for days.*"

"What the fuck is going on?"

"It's my phone," Bec says, her face scrunched up tight.

"What?"

"MY PHONE!"

"Were you watching porn while you're driving? Bec that's so dangerous!"

"No, I would never," she shouts, "It's an audiobook."

"Yes baby, yes, I'm a dirty little whore for your monster cock."

"Lalalalalalaaaaaaa!" Bec starts up her wailing again and I can't get over the shock of hearing such dirty words bounce around the car. This is why she's screaming?

"Well, they don't have books like this at the library."

"It's a dark romance. Please, just find it and shut it off."

I look around her feet for her phone while the narrator fills in more of the picture.

She clenched around his mammoth tool, her screaming moans carrying for miles as he ravaged her raw against the old oak tree.

I cannot believe her with this smut. "Oh my god, Bec, you're a filthbag."

"Oh god. Kill me. Just leave me here to perish. Let the wolves take me."

"We don't have wolves in this country." Her story blares on.

He came with a roar, unleashing a violent torrent inside her with such force that his knees buckled and he fell to the floor. She didn't care, impaled on his heavy shaft she rode him like he was a wild bull and she was a champion cowgirl.

"You were born to ride this dick. Take it, take it," he growled.

"He growled?" I burst out laughing.

"Ahhhhhh. Find my fucking phone, Renn. Please. Please?"

I know how inappropriate it is, but damn, the sweet sound of her begging over this smut is doing things to me beneath my uniform.

The rear door has popped open, bent under the force of the crash. I wrap my hands around the gnarled metal and pry it open further, the hinges creaking apart. I dip my head to look inside, more moans screaming from her phone. Finally I locate it in the rear footwell, wedged under the seat. Tapping the screen, I'm faced with the brooding scowl of a topless, tattooed man. I can't stop myself from laughing again at the sight of the book cover as I move back round to her door.

"*Wrecked By You*. You're listening to a book called *Wrecked By You*?"

"*When I'm done with this pussy you'll be ruined for all men. Tell me who this sweet pussy belongs to. Tell me!*" *he roared.*

"Just shut it off!" Bec screams, and I press the stop button. "Oh, thank god. Now get me out of here. Please Rennie, I'm scared. I'm really scared."

Her voice wobbles. *Fuck.* I can't stand seeing her like this.

"Were you knocked unconscious?"

"No. I don't think so."

Behind me the guys prep the extraction kit; the cutters and spreaders we use for accidents like this, but that will take too long. I need her out of there now.

"Bec, keep your hands over your face." She does as she's told and I pry the driver door open too, grunting as the metal bends beneath the heavy limb of the tree that is blocking most of my access. I push up underneath it with my back and it's just enough, I can get her from here. I crouch back down and reach my arm around behind her lower back. Gripping her hips, I manage to shift her bum out sideways so I can pull her clear from the space.

I slide one arm around her waist and the other cups beneath her thighs. Glass falls all around her as I keep her tight to my chest and carefully pull her out. Finally free, l step back and drop to the floor in a spot clear of the wreckage.

"Alistair, what the hell are you doing?" the Watch Manager shouts, but I don't give a fuck.

"I've got her. She's fine, she's fine." I pull Bec closer and she curls into a ball in my lap. Relief washes over me and finally I take a proper breath. Looking back at her car, I can't believe she ever fit into that tiny space. She's lucky to be alive, but she's safe with me now and that's all that matters. I hold her face in my hands, look into her eyes, and stroke her cold cheek.

"You're OK, you're OK, I've got you, I won't let you go," I whisper, and Bec bursts into tears.

5

Rennie

"No, I haven't been able to see her yet, but I'm not leaving here until I do."

After several calls and messages, I've managed to track down Louise and Mike, Bec's parents, to their campervan in Croatia. My mum and dad are just as shocked as they are, and they've all gathered around the phone for updates. It's taken twenty minutes to fill them in with our dads throwing questions my way, our mums bursting into tears and consoling each other.

"My baby," Louise sobs in my mum's arms.

"She was awake when the ambulance left, Mrs Charlton, I'm sure she's OK." I'm trying to be as reassuring as I can, but the truth is my heart rate is flying and I'm pacing the waiting room floor. I need news as much as they do.

"Alistair, I'm looking up flights," her dad waves his iPad around in the background, "we'll come home right away."

"Let's wait and see how she is," I say. "You know she'll be upset if you all change your plans for her."

An only child, Bec's always been close with her parents, and she told me it took a lot to convince them she'd manage on her own while they took this trip. I know they're just looking out for their daughter, but it pisses me off how much everyone still treats Bec like a kid.

"I'm looking for Rebecca Charlton's next of kin," a male voice calls.

"That's me." I stand and the doctor takes in my uniform, confused. "Well, I have her parents on the phone. They're abroad."

"And you are?"

"Her friend. Her oldest friend," I blurt out. *Go on, try and stop me from seeing her, I dare you.*

"It's fine," her dad says, squeezing into frame. I hold my phone out for the doc to see. "Let him through."

"Are you someone who could take her home?" the doctor asks.

"Yes," I nod. "Absolutely."

"OK, follow me."

"I'll call you back as soon as I can," I say to her folks.

"Give our girl a hug and tell her we love her."

"Of course, Mr Charlton."

"How many times do I have to tell you it's Mike? Now go."

The hospital corridor feels a mile long. The final stretch is like wading through wet sand. I'm shown to her end cubicle and I rush to her side, taking her hand in both of mine. She looks so helpless lying propped up in bed. Her right arm is wrapped up in a sling, her foot in a padded boot elevated on two pillows. They've cleaned her face up a little, but she looks pale and exhausted and no fucking wonder with what she's been through today.

Careful not to hurt her more, I slide my arm behind her back and lean in against her, my face pressed to her hair.

"This is from your mum and dad," I lie. "And they said to tell you they love you."

"Oh god, you rang them?"

"Their only child is in a hospital bed. Your dad would kill me if I didn't tell him what was going on." The idea is laughable. I've probably had a good foot on Mr Charlton since I was sixteen, but I've known him my whole life and he's a man I respect.

"OK, that's enough hugging for now," the doctor interrupts and I hate him for it, but do as I'm told. "She's taken a bit of a beating." *No shit Sherlock, I was there.*

"I'm fine," Bec insists, throwing me a wonky grin that looks quite the opposite of fine.

"She's had some pain relief," the doctor says.

"Oh no, a needle?" I look down at her arm, scanning for a cannula. "She's afraid of needles."

"No, just co-codamol," he clarifies.

"Phew," we both say at the same time.

Back in 2004, the year 9 pupils of Manor Road Community School lined up in alphabetical order to get our BCG vaccinations. A mass operation, we were called two at a time into the school hall where the second I saw a needle, I fell out of my chair.

After coming round, I was given a glass of water then shown through to a low bed in the nurse's office. They covered me with a blanket and told me to stay put until someone came to take me home.

A small voice piped up from across the room, and when I blinked my vision back into focus I'd seen her there, laying on her side on another cot bed, wrapped in a thin blanket.

"Did you faint too?" she asked.

There was no point in lying. Whatever bullshit I might have made up, Bec would have seen right through it.

"Did you know you're afraid of needles?" she'd asked and I'd shaken my head. "Me neither."

"I think they've forgotten about me," Bec had said after a while. "My mum would normally come right away."

The entire afternoon passed, and even now I couldn't tell you what we spoke about. All I know is that we stayed in our beds, facing each other, talking and laughing until we could barely breathe. When I nipped out to go to the bathroom, I considered going back to class, but in the end I crawled back into my bed and wished it was closer to hers.

When the school bell rang, still no one had come. We figured we didn't want to get locked in, so we just left. I'd walked her home that day, no great effort when she lived across the road, but we both instinctively turned to take the long way back, through the woodland and out along the fields at the edge of town.

When we were little, our mums walked us to school together every day, but once we were allowed to walk on our own to secondary school, Bec had started leaving early to go with her friends. I'd been butthurt about it and complained to my mum, who'd told me friends would come and go, but Bec would always be in my life. It hadn't made any sense to me at the time, but I guess it has worked out that way.

I still remember the look on her face when we got to her house that day and I accidentally said *"See you tomorrow baby"*, instead of *"See you tomorrow, Bec."* I'd nearly died of embarrassment, but she'd just smiled as she walked backwards up the path to her door.

I'd been so distracted thinking about her smile, I hadn't even noticed the new family moving in next door to her.

"My car, Rennie," Bec says with a pained look on her face. "Will she be OK?"

Jesus christ, the woman nearly lost her life, and she's worried about her car? I don't know whether to be mad or to laugh. She's been driving her Grandad's ancient Ford Cortina since he stopped and she looks after it just as well as he did. It met a cruel fate, but I couldn't give a shit about that right now. The only thing I care about is her. I rub my thumb back and forth in her palm.

"I don't think so sweetheart, those old cars aren't as strong as new ones. The roof took the full weight of the tree trunk."

"It sounds like you were very lucky," the doctor says, tapping away at their notes on a screen.

"She was," I say. "It missed her by a few inches." My eyes don't leave hers when I reach up without thinking and smooth her hair away from her face. Tears fill her eyes and I wipe them away before they can fall. I don't think I could bear seeing her cry right now.

"Does it hurt?"

"More emotionally than anything else. I loved her."

"I know you did. I know."

"Is the road blocked? What about the wedding?" Even in this condition she's thinking about others.

"My guys will have it cleared in no time, but I think most of them are coming from the South side so it will be fine. Don't worry about it."

"I'm embarrassed," she says, pulling her hand away and biting her thumb. I know she's not referring to the accident and I'm not surprised she feels embarrassed. Goody-two shoes Bec being rumbled as a smut fiend was not something I ever could have predicted would happen when I got out of bed this morning.

"You've got nothing to be embarrassed about. It'll be a great story for the grandkids." *Jesus, what the fuck am I saying? Grandkids? With Bec?* Suddenly it's all I see. Me and her, Sunday lunch, an entire brood around the dinner table, young and old and happy as pigs in shit.

She stares into my eyes, and I wonder if she sees it too. Her lips part, then close, then open again. I'm dying to hear whatever she has to say, but the doctor interrupts our moment.

"So Rebecca, you've got a sprained ankle, a sprained wrist, and a touch of whiplash. Good news is they're all mild cases."

"Oh, thank god. Thank god." I turn to face the doctor. "So nothing is broken?"

"No sir, nothing is broken."

"You're sure? You've x-rayed her? What about internal bleeding?"

"We're sure," he says, doing shit all to relieve my concerns. "Now Rebecca, you'll need to keep your arm in a sling for a few days, and keep the weight off your foot for at least 48 hours. Icing it a few times a day will help with any swelling, but never more than twenty minutes."

"Really?" Bec rolls her eyes. "That'll be tricky. I have a shop to run."

"Really really. The more you rest up now, the quicker you'll be back on your feet. I'm also going to give you a soft neck collar, but this is just really for a few days. Regular painkillers and gentle movement when you feel up to it will be more effective than keeping it still, but I know it will feel a little tender for a few days."

"OK," she huffs.

"I'll type up your discharge notes and a prescription for you to collect. Someone will bring you crutches and a wheelchair to take you to the main entrance. Do you have a way to get home?"

"I'll take her," I say before she has a chance to protest, and the doctor disappears behind the curtain.

"Renn—" she tries to sit herself up a little straighter. "You can't, you're working."

"I'm done, boss wouldn't let me come back. I drove straight here."

"Why?"

"I had to be with you." Her face twists and I can't tell if she's happy or in pain.

"Are you sure? I can call a taxi."

"Bec, you scared the shit out of me today. I'm not letting you out of my sight." Her face softens and when she nods in agreement, I press a kiss to her forehead. I can't help myself, and I can't let anything else happen to her.

6

Rennie

"**B**ec, this is ridiculous."

"Shut up."

As hard-headed as ever, she won't accept my help. She can't put any weight on her ankle, yet she insists on having a go at climbing the narrow, steep stairs to her flat. She manages to jump up two steps before she stumbles. I'm right there to catch her.

"You can't stay here," I say. Sliding one arm around her waist, I turn her and heave her up into a firefighter's lift. She yelps in protest, her crutches clattering against the wall. I try to ignore the fact that my arm is wedged between her legs. Legs that are currently squeezing me tight.

At the top of the stairs I set her down so she can find her keys in her bag. Sliding the key in the lock proves to be a challenge with her dominant hand in the sling. I reach out and try to take them from her, but she elbows me away, then winces at the movement.

"Let me help you."

"I'm *fine*," she spits, throwing the door open so hard it hits the wall. She shuffles her way along the hallway and into her bedroom, but the wall takes most of her weight. I lean against the doorframe and watch as she tries to figure out how to cross the space between the doorway and her bed. It's only a few feet, but with nothing to lean into, it must seem like an ocean.

I pick her up again and, fortunately, she's less resistant next time.

"Bec, you can't stay here by yourself. I know your ankle will feel better in a few days, but right now you need to keep the weight off and do as little as possible."

"I'll manage."

I shake my head and mutter under my breath. "So stubborn."

I make a pile of pillows in the centre of her bed, and help her sit back against them. While she tries to get comfortable, I pull a weekend bag from the top of her wardrobe. I set it down on the foot of her bed and look around her room, trying to figure out where she keeps everything.

"What are you doing?"

"You're coming to stay with me until you're better. Tell me what you need."

"I am not," she says, her voice raised. This is ridiculous.

"You fucking are." She baulks at the volume of my reaction, and I take a deep breath to calm myself down. "I apologise for swearing at you, but this is not up for debate. You can't get up and down the stairs, Bec."

"I'll ask my mum to come back."

"And ruin the trip they've been planning for so long? Have you forgotten the PowerPoint presentation with their itinerary, because I haven't. That thing took hours and they've still got miles to go."

"Alyssa can help me."

"I've already spoken to her. She'll be covering for you in the shop until you're better. You can't stay here on your own."

I pace back and forward at the foot of her bed, my head full of worst-case scenarios. "What if you fall going to the bathroom? What if there's a fire? I can't leave you trapped here. My place is all on one level. I'll set you up in the spare room, and I'll take a few days off to help you recover."

"No, you can't do that for me."

I huff out a sigh and take a seat next to her on the edge of her bed. "Listen, I know you're this super badass woman who can do everything herself, but I'd feel so much better if I can keep an eye on you. Please, Bec, you need to let me help you."

"Why?" she frowns.

"Because it's my fault."

She frowns. She's so cute when she frowns. "What, you're like the god of storms or something?"

"No, but I knew how bad it could be. I shouldn't have let you go out in this weather."

"It's my job. I wouldn't have let you stop me."

I bury my hands in the pockets of my hoodie and stare at the floor.

"Renn, you can't possibly believe this was your fault. It was a freak accident. Please tell me you know that, right?"

"I know, it's just—" What's the point in trying to explain it to her when I can't even explain it to myself? I'm normally pretty good at compartmentalising work and my personal life. Firefighters have to be. We can't be thinking about the last job when we're on to the next, and it's a slippery slope to come home and revisit every detail over and over.

So why can't I shake the panicked feeling I had when I first saw Bec's car?

I thought I'd lost her, and worst-case scenarios are not something I do. The training kicks in, I assess a situation with the information I have at the time and, sure, we run through potential outcomes, but I do not allow myself to think the worst.

I keep replaying the look on her face when she saw me, and the relief I felt when I realised she was alive. I'm not ready to unpack either of those things.

I have this need for control, I've always had it. I don't like surprises and I don't like chaos. I like order. I like to tick things off lists and stick to plans and Bec getting hurt was never in any fucking plan. Yes, I know I broke protocol when I dragged her out of her car, and I know I'll probably get written up for it. It will be my first ever infringement, but I don't care. In that moment, I had to have her safe in my arms. This is not order and control, and it's thrown me for a loop.

Bec stares at me, waiting for an answer I can't give her. I turn away and leave the room to take a look around her flat.

When we were kids, this place was mostly empty. Her Grandpa used it for his office and storage, and she's done a beautiful job of turning it into a home. It's small but cosy thanks to the carpet she had fitted, and the thick, long curtains I helped her hang. Too many trinkets and things for my liking but that's just Bec's personal taste. All these bloody candles are a fire hazard.

A book with a cutesy cover sits open on the sofa and I pick it up and scan a couple of pages. This is not cute. This is a couple going at in in an elevator and it is absolute filth. I didn't even know they made books this dirty. I need to get a grip of my dick. No, not that, the opposite of that.

I fold up the blankets on her sofa and plump the cushions. Three half-full glasses of water sit abandoned on her coffee table. I tip them into her houseplants, take them through to her small kitchen and wash them in the sink.

"When did you last check your smoke alarms?" I call out.

"Every Monday morning, just like I promised," comes her reply. Good girl. I like knowing she does what I tell her to do. I wonder if I'm on her mind when she does it?

I check the one in her kitchen again anyway, reaching up to depress the test button. After the beeping stops, I hear her shout. "Do you not believe me?"

"Never hurts to check twice."

I really don't see how she can manage here. There's a woven rug on the kitchen floor that's a trip hazard even at the best of times, let alone on crutches. The windows at the front of the house are original and she'll need to reach up high to open them. I've seen her balancing on a little footstool to do it. And those stairs are narrow, dimly lit, with no handrail. Fucking ridiculous. I'll install one as soon as I can.

In her bathroom, I shove everything on the little shelf into her toiletries bag and storm back through to her room. "You're not staying here. So tell me what you need, or you can spend a week wearing my clothes."

"Fine," she scoffs. "But I forbid you from taking time off work."

"*Fine,*" I scoff back. "I'm on day shift tomorrow, then two nights, then four days off anyway." I can't help but grin. She hasn't won that easily.

"Fine. Get my jogging bottoms." She points me in the direction of the wardrobe, the second drawer for t-shirts, the third for pyjamas. I have to steady myself against the top of the cabinet when I open her underwear drawer. Crammed full of these bright, lacy, little things, my mind floods with the most incredible images. Bec in this scrap of underwear. Spread out on my bed. Me peeling them off with my teeth.

A lick of shame crawls up my spine. I'm a perverted arsehole intruding into her most personal space. My shame spirals into a heavy knot in my stomach when a thought occurs to me. Who does Bec wear these for? And why do I want to make sure no man ever sees her underwear again?

I grab a bunch in my fist and see stars when her wand vibrator reveals itself. I'm learning a lot of things about Rebecca Charlton today, and all of them are torturing me in the dick.

"Do you need this?" I ask, holding it up for her to see.

"Oh piss off," she whines, burying her face in the crook of her good elbow. "And shut that drawer!"

I put it back, but it's too late. I've seen it now, and the rest. The image of her naked, touching herself, riding against the buzzing head, is already scorching itself into my brain. I picture her listening to that audiobook and driving herself wild.

"I can't believe that filth you were listening to in your car," I say, closing the drawer and dropping her underwear into the bag.

Bec's cheeks are rosy red. "Look, Renn, I know you're a nice guy. I'm sorry if it was offensive to you. Please, can we agree that you'll never mention it again? I'm already half dead from embarrassment."

She doesn't need to be embarrassed. If anything, it piqued my interest. I want to know everything she's into now. "I'm not offended. I just had no idea you were into that stuff."

"Yeah, well, I don't exactly write it on the sandwich board outside the shop."

"You should," I laugh. "Business would triple."

Back at home, I ditch her bags first, then carry Bec in from the car. Half the curtains in the street are probably twitching behind me. It's getting late, so I head straight for the guest bedroom and lay her on the bed. My dick twitches behind my fly. Though this is how many of our fantasies about Bec begin, these circumstances are far from sexual. *Not now, dick.*

I get to work plumping pillows for her to rest against, and bring water to her bedside table. I set out the prescription we collected before we left the hospital, plug in her phone charger, then dig her e-reader out of her bag. Finally, I grab an ice pack from my freezer, sit down on the bed, and settle her legs across my lap.

"I hope the room is OK for you," I say, wrapping the pack around her ankle. "I know it's not exactly up to your sex dungeon standards. I could probably install a swing if you need one?" *Why am I torturing myself like this?*

I don't miss the way she blushes and looks away from me. "It's fine."

"You sure? Want me to order a—"

"Rennie quit it!" she snaps. "I cannot stay here if you're just going to tease me all week."

Little does Bec know, teasing her for a week is my idea of heaven. I don't know why I can't quit ribbing her about this. "I'm sorry, I'm just seeing you in a totally different light."

"What do you mean?"

"I just didn't think you were the type of woman who was into all that dirty talk."

"And what type of woman did you think I was?" she says, her head cocked as little as her neck brace allows, her mouth pressed into a tight line.

Shit. This is a trap. "I don't know. "I scratch the back of my neck and stare at the floor to buy myself some time. "I guess I just didn't know you had a darker side, that's all."

"Well looks can be deceiving," she says, glaring at me.

What the hell does that mean?

7

Bec

I'm awake long before I consider getting out of bed. Yesterday I thought I felt OK, but today everything hurts. I must have been running on some adrenaline high. Now that it's all out of my system, I feel heavy and achy all over. A headache pounds out a new thought with every thump.

My beautiful car.

I didn't make it back to work.

Was everything OK with the wedding?

I slept in Rennie's house.

I'll need to find another car for deliveries.

I need to open the shop this morning.

Who will make the sandwiches?

There's so much to do.

I slept in Alistair Frickin Rendall's house.

It's safe to say the past twenty-four hours have been some of the worst of my life. Rennie rescuing me, Rennie hearing my audiobook, Rennie coming to my hospital bedside, insisting I come home with him, helping me to the bathroom, and then into bed. Having your crush remove your trousers because you can't manage by yourself is the opposite of sexy. I feel embarrassed, and pathetic.

I've never been a good patient. I'm far too stubborn and strong-willed to let anyone do anything for me, and I certainly never ask for help. Being here is so far out of my comfort zone, even if I will accept that I'd have lasted ten minutes at home on my own before calling him back.

I try to sit up, then wince, momentarily forgetting that my wrist can't take any pressure. I looped the sling off over my head in the night because I was worried I'd somehow strangle myself with it. There's a knock at the door and I check I'm decent. Phew, no rogue nipples or underwear on display.

"Come in."

"Good morning." He leans against the doorframe, careful not to cross the threshold. Showered and dressed in dark grey trousers and a tight black t-shirt, the sight of him looking so fresh and clean makes me feel like a swamp thing in comparison. I must stink, my hair probably still has leaves in it, and my breath is almost certainly toxic. "How are you feeling?"

"Like a tree fell on my car and nearly crushed me to death inside it," I say without a hint of sarcasm. His face is deadpan. "Too soon?" I grimace.

"I'm just making breakfast. Shall I bring you some in bed or do you want some help to come through for it?"

"Just give me a few minutes and I'll come through." I'd like to make myself a little more presentable before sitting down to breakfast with the man of my dreams.

"Call out when you're ready and I'll help you. I don't want you moving on your own any more than is absolutely necessary." He turns to leave and I roll my eyes. "Don't roll your eyes at me, Bec."

How does he do that?

Much to my annoyance, he's right. It's tough to sit up in bed, tougher to get out of it. I manage to use the crutches to hop through to the bathroom and pee, but I can only use my one good hand, and

I panic about toppling over the whole time. Then Rennie would find me on the bathroom floor, pants around my ankles, covered in my own piss. No wonder he finds me so irresistible.

Oh wait, that's just in my head.

I consider crawling through to the kitchen, dragging my ankle behind me, but turning up to breakfast like the girl from The Ring would probably be even worse than accepting a little help.

After flushing, I lean my hip against the sink to wash my face, then rake my fingers through my hair. Left-handed toothbrushing is a mountain I'll have to climb later. Dried blood has crusted around my hairline. I don't remember bleeding, but when I part my hair, sure enough, there's a tender spot with a scab already forming.

I try to remember hitting my head, but it all happened so fast. The car swung, the tree fell, and I was trapped.

It's slowly dawning on me just how lucky I am. This wasn't just a little accident. In the mirror I catch my face shifting and a ball of sadness pushes up out of my lungs, filling my throat.

"Rennie," I call out, and he's by my side in a heartbeat. I try to blink the tears away, but it's too late, and a sob breaks free. He spins me on my good foot, and lifts me to sit on the edge of the vanity unit, crowding in between my legs, wrapping me in his arms, and holding me to his chest. I'd be dry humping the life out of him if I wasn't processing trauma right this second.

"Oh Bec, oh honey, it's OK, you're OK. You'll be OK."

He holds me for ages, one warm hand stroking up and down my back, until slowly the panic subsides.

After we eat, he stands at my back while I wash my hands at the kitchen sink. His arms float on either side of me, ready to steady any wobbles. I wish he'd wrap those arms around my waist, pull my back against his chest and press his dick against my arse. Maybe I'd wiggle a little against him to tease him, to get him hard until he—

"Bed or sofa?" I feel him whisper against the back of my neck. Tingles shoot down my spine, spreading through my limbs to the tips of my fingers and toes. My breath catches in my chest.

"For what?"

"For resting." *Oh, that. Boring.*

"Sofa please."

Rennie helps me through to the living room, then fusses around me like a mother hen. Piles of pillows, extra blankets, three bottles of water, a basket full of snacks in reach. I don't know when he did all this.

"I'm sorry I'll be gone all day, but I'll leave the patio door unlocked and have a couple of people pop in and check on you. OK?"

I told Rennie I'd accept his offer of help and a place to stay while I can't manage stairs to my flat, but under no circumstances is he to take time off work to look after me. I can't be that much of a burden.

"Who?" I don't really want anyone to see me like this. It's bad enough that he has, but I don't have the energy to protest.

"I'll leave it as a surprise."

"Please no, not the tennis mums?"

"No," he smirks. "I think you've suffered enough." He fusses around a little, plumping cushions he's already plumped.

"So here's the remote." He sets it on the armrest next to me. "TV is all fairly self-explanatory. Do you want me to put some porn on for you?" he laughs. *When will this torment end?*

"Fuck off Renn. Go to work."

"OK, OK," he says, hands held up to his chest, palms facing out as he backs away from me. "I'm gone."

"Be safe. And bring ice-cream home with you."

Rennie has barely been gone an hour when Alyssa appears at the patio door, arms laden with flowers and gift bags.

"NO!" she shouts at me through the glass pane when I move to get up and open it for her. I sink back down into pillow mountain.

"Oh my god, look at the state of you," she says, sliding the door closed behind her. Her no BS attitude is actually quite refreshing after Rennie's "you look fine, everything is *fiiine*" approach.

"Right, these flowers are from me, and these are from Janet and Andrew." Janet and Andrew are Rennie's parents, they must have called in an order, and they've already texted a few times to make sure I'm feeling at home. She lays them down on the coffee table next to my leg and I wonder if Rennie even owns a vase. "Then I've got recuperation gifts from Graeme and Liz, the whole team at David's, Moira, Louise, and all the beauty girls at Lucie's, too. Oh and a gift basket from Mrs Marshall. She's horrified."

Mrs Marshall is head of the town council, and along with her, Alyssa has named practically every small business owner on the high street. News of my predicament clearly spread fast.

"It's mostly snacks for while you're laid up, and if it seems like a couple of chocolates are missing, don't blame me." I will blame her, the sneaky bitch.

"So the whole town is talking about it. Rennie rushing to your side, pulling you from the burning blaze. What a stud."

"Please, that is not what happened. There was no fire." *Though I can't deny the stud part.*

"I know, but you know how this town is. We've been overdue a bit of excitement. The last big thing was when Mr Marshall's basement flooded. Though come to think of it, that was mainly because Rennie was soaking wet."

"Oh jeez, as if we needed anything else to add to his list of heroics."

"Is it true he caught you watching porn?"

"Oh my god, NO!" I throw my head back but it barely moves with this stupid beige bastard strapped around my neck. "I was listening to an audiobook. He just happened to appear during a pivotal scene."

"Shit babe, how mortifying." Alyssa is no stranger to spicy romance herself, and we've spent many a slow afternoon singing the praises of our latest book boyfriends.

"Please tell me about work. Tell me the weddings were OK."

"I haven't heard a peep from either of the weddings, which means they were fine. Today was your day off anyway, and when I get in and open up, I'll arrange cover for you for the rest of the week."

"I forgot my laptop. Can you head up to my flat and pick it up after you close?"

"What do you need it for?"

"Work! I have orders to submit, invoices to pay, wedding enquiries to book in."

"I refuse to let you do any of those things. I'll handle it."

The idea of sitting on the sofa all day and not doing any work is making me feel itchy. I've barely spent a day away from the shop since I was a child. I don't know if I can just let someone else take over for me.

"What about cheese and wine tonight?"

"I'm hosting. You know I wish you'd let me do those anyway."

"What about the sandwiches? Nobody else has ever made the sandwiches."

This is not about the sandwiches. It's not even the work, it's the place. The calming green walls, the window displays I spend hours tinkering with, it's my shop and my home, and I miss it.

"Don't be such a control freak, Bec," she says, patting my leg. "I've seen you do these things a million times. I've got it. Let us look after you the way you look after everyone else."

"Do you need anything before I go?"

"Actually, while you're here, I have a huge favour to ask."

"Anything. What do you need?"

"Do you have time to help me have a quick bath? I'm so gross, and I can't ask Rennie to do this for me."

"Oh, I bet Rennie would love to wash your dirty bits," she laughs as she heads for the bathroom.

When the water is ready, she helps me along the hallway and I start to clam up. Alyssa is my friend, but she's also my employee, and this is not a normal request from your boss. I try to push down my embarrassment by reminding myself that I'm a mess and I was in a car accident. I genuinely need this help.

Getting me into the tub is a mission and a half. Alyssa has to remove my sling and my ankle support, undress me, then help lower me into the water without getting herself soaked. I soap up a washcloth and clean where I can reach, but she does my back and grabs a jug from the kitchen to wash my hair. The heat of the water is heaven and I can feel some of my aches being soothed already.

"So what's it like staying with Rennie?" she asks, rubbing conditioner into the lengths of my hair. I forgot to ask him to pack mine, so now I'll be cursed with smelling like him all night. "Does he walk around in his pants? Does he do naked yoga? Does he eat whipped cream straight from the can?"

Don't think about it, don't think about it.

Too late, I'm thinking about it. Rennie. Naked. With a can of whipped cream in his hand, threatening to use it on me. I'm also naked in this scenario. *Snap out of it, Rebecca.*

"What the hell is going on in your head? Why is everyone so obsessed with him?"

"Come on, you know how hot it is," Alyssa says. "The big hunky firefighter rescuing you. It's like something from a book."

"He was just doing his job." I swallow thickly and squeeze my eyes shut while she rinses my hair.

I've never told anyone about my crush on Rennie. In fact, I generally refrain from engaging in conversation about him at all. When people mention his name in the shop, I just smile and carry on working. When they ask me if he's single, I say *"I wouldn't know"* and change the subject.

It's just a little crush, and that's all it's ever been. I know Rennie would never think of me that way. I'm also certain that, despite his appearance doing utterly wild things to my insides, he'd be so nice in bed I'd barely make a dent in the list of the things I want him to do to me.

My fantasies about Alistair Rendall are bordering on unhinged. Rennie rescuing me from various plights. Rennie climbing through my bedroom window and ravishing me in the night. Taking me here, there, and everywhere. Rennie turning his firehose on me and blasting my clothes off. Don't tell me the science, I don't want to know.

Unfortunately, my rescue scenarios never extended to being pulled from the wreckage of my beloved car. No, that was never the way I imagined his hands on me.

"Well, you've not even been here 24 hours," Alyssa says. "If it turns out he does do naked yoga, promise me I'll be the first to know."

"I promise," I fib. No way would I tell a soul. I would take those memories to my dirty grave, with a thousand orgasms along the way.

8

Rennie

Why did I open my big mouth? I was just teasing, and now I can't get the thought of Bec watching porn in my house out of my head. After discovering the stuff she reads and listens to, I'm desperate to know more about what she likes.

Having her in my home is a bad idea. It's one thing to fantasise about having her in my bed. Quite another to have her sleeping on the other side of the wall.

It's too late now, though. I offered my help without a second thought, not realising I'd be putting myself through a week of torture. I can hardly send her home. She's had enough hurt. I won't hurt her more.

Fortunately, the morning has been quiet on shift. Unfortunately, that means there's plenty of time for the crew to ask me questions about yesterday and make jokes about Bec and the situation we found her in. Turns out I'm not the only one who was shocked by what they heard.

We spent our afternoon on a call out to a barn fire, and now I'm rounding out the last of my shift with extra time in the gym. I'm almost done when the Chief Fire Officer, who happens to be my Uncle Jeff, pokes his head in.

"Alistair, a word."

I follow him down the corridor and into his office. Not much has changed in here over the years. I got to visit a few times when I was a boy, and later when I became more serious about joining the fire service, but this is the first time I've been in for a bollocking.

"Sit," he says, and I perch on the edge of the office chair across the desk from him. "How's Rebecca doing?"

"She's fine." My knee jiggles up and down and I lean forward, pressing my elbow into it to make it stop. "Sprained ankle, sprained wrist, bit of whiplash. She'll be OK as long as she rests properly."

"Oh, she won't like that. Did I hear that she's staying with you?"

"Yes Sir, that's right. She can't manage the stairs to her flat on crutches."

"Something going on between you two I don't know about?"

"No, Sir." He glares at me for an uncomfortably long time.

"So about yesterday. I hear you broke protocol about fifty different ways. I hear you approached the scene without appropriate caution or protective gear. And I hear you pulled her from the wreckage without securing the crash site and before an ambulance was on scene. What the fuck is wrong with you?"

"I'm sorry Sir, I apologise. I shouldn't have done what I did, but I needed to get her out of there as quickly as possible."

"What if she'd suffered a spinal injury?"

"She hadn't."

"And how did you know? You been moonlighting as a paramedic?"

"I just knew."

"Do you love her?"

"What?" *What is he talking about?* "I... er—"

"Listen Alistair, I've been in this job long enough to know there are only two reasons a man behaves like you did yesterday. Either they're losing their mind over the pressures of the job, or they're losing their mind over a woman. I hope for both our sakes that in this case it's the latter."

"I—" I genuinely don't know what to say. *Love? Bec? Is that what this is? No, that's fucking crazy.*

"Alistair, you know me. I'm not much of a romantic, which is how you'll know I mean it when I say, go home and tell that woman how you really feel about her."

I mean, sure, I like Bec. I've always had a thing for her, but love? No, it's just a misguided, wholly unrequited, physical attraction. A teenage crush I've never had a chance to get out of my system.

There have been a few women over the years. Not many, not for long, and especially not from around here. Not since Sophie.

The truth of it is, no matter how good the sex is, I always have to hold back, and it leaves me feeling empty. No matter how hard I try not to let her into my head, there's always a moment where I picture Bec and then I feel like a scumbag.

Bec is not a woman who you fuck around with. She's a woman you'd make love to. She deserves someone who'll treat her right, make her their world, fill her belly with babies, and live happily ever after. Not someone like me, a monster who has imagined leaving her marked, getting so deep inside her she can't sit without wincing.

Her pureness makes me feel like poison in comparison. She's beautiful, smart, runs her own business, and half this town along with it. She'll do anything for anyone but take no shit along the way. She's not going to get on her knees for me. She's not going to let me do half the things I stroke myself off thinking about. I'm a strong guy, and if I can't control myself when I'm just thinking about her, I don't have a hope in hell of being restrained in person. If I hurt her, I'd never forgive myself.

No, I can't love Bec. I just can't. If I love her, I have to leave. Someone perfect for her will come along. It's only a matter of time. I'll have to see them dating, holding hands in the street, kissing in the pub. I'll have to keep a straight face when she tells me he's moving in, shows me the ring he'll buy her, and watch her live her happy, perfect life with him and not me.

I won't be able to bear it. And that guy will never be me. I'm fucked either way.

"I don't know what I'm gonna do with you Alistair but, for now, you're dismissed," I hear my uncle say.

"I'm not in love with Bec," I stand abruptly, my chair hurtling backwards. "And I want a transfer."

9

Bec

After Alyssa left, I took a nap, then spent the rest of the day watching Friends reruns under a blanket, and hobbling to the toilet every few hours. I considered taking a nap in Rennie's bed, but worried he might come home and find me there like some sort of nympho Goldilocks.

Being alone in his house should feel weird, but it's not. I just need to be careful I'm not making myself too comfortable.

The snack basket was decimated by lunch, just in time for Sarah to swing by with a fresh loaf, her Floury Godmother bike trailer laden with deliveries.

"I can't stop long, but I thought this would get you through the afternoon."

"You are an angel."

"I've sliced and buttered it for you already. Extra butter, you know it's a superfood," she said, blowing me a kiss as she closed the door behind her.

Mum rang me in the afternoon to check in, but it was a brief call before she, Dad, and Mr and Mrs Rendall headed to some private art tour with a painter they met last night. Quite the bohemian life they're living on the road.

June and Mary, Rennie's neighbours, brought me a lamb casserole and mashed potatoes for dinner. They were keen to stay and help, but since they are pushing 80, I thanked them and told them to have a lovely evening. Of course, they had plenty to say as they headed out the door.

"Is Alistair looking after you properly?"

"Do you have everything you need?"

"When will Alistair be home? Shall we stay until he gets back?"

"Thank goodness Alistair is looking after you. You really need a husband for these sorts of things, dear."

Thatch Cross is full of people like June and Mary. They love gossip, the juicier the better, and seem to have sources everywhere. I'm not an idiot, I know I'm this week's hot topic. I understand everyone wants to hear all about it, but I hate being the centre of attention.

They are also people who pressed pound coins into my palm when I was a little girl, folded my fingers around them, and told me not to spend it all at once. My piggy bank had to be emptied so often the ladies at the building society gave me a second one.

Yes, my parents raised me, along with my Gramps, but these people bore witness to all of it. They cheered when I got exam results, bought me Christmas presents, and gave me gifts when I moved into my own house. They're an extended family and I'll never take it for granted how lucky I am to have so many people looking out for me.

I loved growing up here, love my shop, and love feeling part of a community. This is a safe place. I know what to expect, nothing ever rocks the boat.

Yet they still see me as a little girl, and I've always felt a strange need to keep up that reputation. Nice, helpful Rebecca. A reliable, friendly face. Part of the furniture.

I never had the travel bug or itchy feet. No calling to do bigger things. But sometimes I wonder, am I really going to live my whole life here in Thatch Cross? I know I shouldn't dwell on it, but I could have died in that accident. I could have died having done nothing with my life. Well, not nothing. My life has had purpose and joy, but for the first time, I'm truly wondering if there could be more out there for me.

I wonder how things would be if I left. Where would I go? What would I do? Who would I meet? What amazing sexual adventures might I have?

Then I remember that I'd miss everything and everyone. A certain hot, ripped firefighter most of all.

10

Bec

I really wish I'd told Rennie to pack my vibrator. Why couldn't I have bashed up my left wrist instead? It's impossible to get off with this wrist guard on and, though I've certainly made a thorough effort with my other hand, the orgasm I desperately crave evades me.

Maybe I broke my vagina in the crash. Why didn't I ask them to x-ray my vagina? That's my best bit!

I've got proper FOMO tonight too, I'm supposed to be hosting our cheese and wine tasting right now. I trust Alyssa to handle it, but I get a social high from being around other people. These hours on Rennie's sofa are blurring together and making me miserable.

Though that bath did me the world of good, I'm still achy. I hate being back in my neck brace, and it turns out that grumpy horny is the worst kind of horny.

When Rennie works day shifts he starts early and finishes late, and even though I could do with an early night, I'm holding out because I want to see him. Maybe a good look at him will give me the sexy ammo I need to get over the edge once I'm in bed. Though since that bed is in the room next to his, I don't think I'll be able to do anything without being heard.

He's already caught me listening to smut. I would have to leave town if he caught me masturbating too.

Though imagine if he did. Imagine if he came home and heard me moaning. Imagine if he watched me through a gap in the door and I opened my eyes to see him getting off too and we both came at exactly the same time. Ooh, or imagine if he burst in and...

I push my left hand into my underwear and try again. I'm slick and close already, but it's useless. Why couldn't I have been born ambidextrous?

My heart leaps into my throat when I hear his key in the door. I yank my hand away, quickly adjusting my clothes and blankets.

"Hey Bec, you home?" he calls out and I roll my eyes.

"Don't be a dick," I shout back. "Where else am I gonna be?" He appears in the living room doorway and I watch him as he ducks into the kitchen with a bag full of groceries. The kitchen island connects the two spaces, and I have a good view of him unpacking.

"I wasn't sure which flavour ice-cream you wanted, so I got three kinds." He crouches to stash them in the freezer, then stands and turns to face me. "Wow, you look... better."

"I think you mean I look clean. Alyssa had to bathe me."

"Oh." His eyes go wide and scrubs at his jawline. "I could have helped you with that." The base of my neck heats at the thought of it.

"How was work?" I ask, shifting to sit up a little higher.

"Rough afternoon. We had a big fire up at the Hillman farm."

"Oh shit, is everyone OK?"

"Yeah, but they lost a building and most of their hay supply."

"That's so awful. I'll send them a gift basket from the shop."

He sets his palms on the kitchen counter and leans into those gorgeous forearms, all thick and corded. I can't help but picture myself between those arms, gripping onto them while he goes to town on me. My gaze drifts up to his biceps, those strong shoulders. I go to my happy place when I imagine licking his throat, kissing his jawline on my way to sinking my teeth into his full lower lip. I read once that the perfect shade of lipstick is one that matches the colour of your nipple and, having had a good look at my own, I now think they match his lips exactly. His lips. My nipples. Hot, wet, sharp teeth. Imagine. Imagine. Imagine.

I moan softly at the thought and then make the mistake of glancing upwards where I find his eyes boring into mine. I blink out of my smutty stupor and fumble for the remote amongst the blankets, somehow flinging it across the room. It crashes to the floor, the batteries bust free from their casing, and scattering across the room.

I move to get up from the sofa and fix it, but it's awkward getting my ankle off the footstool and I end up slumping onto my side.

"No!" Rennie shouts, rounding the counter at lightning speed. "You stay right there."

He rushes to kneel in front of me, lifting me with those big, warm hands until I'm back in a seated position. He cups the back of my leg, lifting it gently back onto the footstool, and the lightest sweep of his thumb has my leg twitching under his touch.

Perched on one knee, I have a sudden vision of him proposing to me. It makes my stomach turn somersaults.

"I'm gonna hop in the shower," he says, standing abruptly. He always showers at the station after his shift and then again when he gets home. He once told me the first gets rid of the dirt and grime, the second gets rid of that deeper layer of smoky musk, the smell that right now is filling my nostrils and driving me wild. I've always loved that smell on him.

"Can you not?"

"Huh?" he doesn't catch my meaning, though why would he? For him this is a nasty side effect of his work, it's me who is the sick perve.

"Can you shower later?" His brow furrows while I figure out how to explain myself. "I kind of like the smoky smell."

"You do?"

"Yeah. I mean, nobody died today, right? You don't smell of death, do you?"

"No, nobody died." Gathering the pieces of the remote from the floor, he takes a seat beside me while he fixes it. He props one foot on the stool next to mine and our legs are so close to touching that I swear I can feel sparks zipping back and forth between us. We watch a few minutes of an old Friends episode in silence before he clocks me, leaning in a little closer to inhale his smoky, woody scent.

"So I'm supposed to just sit here while you sniff me?" he laughs.

"I'm not sniffing you!"

"Yes you are, you pervert." *Rumbled.*

"OK fine, I am. Just let me smell you and stop judging me."

"Be my guest, creep." He spreads his arms along the back of the sofa and tips his head back, inviting me in. My booted ankle is still outstretched as I shuffle round to face him side on. I press my face to his chest and take a deep inhale, letting the deep notes of burnt hay fill my lungs. I must look insane, but I'm so drunk with lust that I don't even care.

"Why do you like it so much?" he asks, his eyes closing softly as he starts to unwind from his day.

"I don't know," I lie.

"It's not a sexy smell for me, it's just the smell of work. I don't even notice it."

"I never said it was sexy." I feel heat blooming in my cheeks.

"Yeah right," he scoffs, turning his face towards me. "Your eyes are rolling back in your head. You're drooling."

"I am not!" I yell, but I wipe my mouth with the back of my hand anyway, just in case. "I think maybe because... it has nice memories for me rather than bad ones."

"Like what?"

Could I tell him? Should I tell him? Fuck it.

"Do you remember that bonfire night when we were kids, where the pyre got out of control?"

"Yeah, that was the first night I got to see my uncle in action."

"Yeah, he and his crew came and put the thing out. We snuck away from the crowd and watched from the edge of the clearing. You were obsessed."

"Yeah," he says, wistfully. "I mean, he was already my hero, but from then I wanted to be just like him."

I get ready to dive over the edge of the cliff. "There was another first that night, too." I bite my lip, I can't believe I'm bringing this up. He lifts his head and turns his body sideways to face me. I search his face for a sign of recognition.

His voice drops, his words slow as they pour from him. "You'll have to jog my memory."

"It's OK, it was just a silly little thing. Forget it." I shake my head and move to turn away, but he grabs my good hand and pulls me back towards him, even closer than before.

"It can't have been that silly if you still remember," he says. With his eyes on mine and fingers resting in my palm, I feel like I'm burning up inside.

"It was the first night I held hands with a boy." A muscle in his jaw ticks and when he swallows, I know he must remember it too.

"With me?"

"Yeah. With you."

It was the winter we turned fourteen and my body and emotions were in overdrive. If I wasn't at school I was moping, skulking around the house and screaming tirades of "you just don't understand me" at my parents every five seconds. How could they? I barely understood myself.

The only place I felt calm was in the shop with my Gramps. He'd let me keep to myself in the back office; do stock takes, process orders, busy work that kept my scowling face away from customers.

Fourteen is a confusing age and there was nothing in my life more confusing than Alistair Rendall, and the way he made me feel. Sometimes I hated him just for existing, and other times I'd wrap myself up in my duvet and close my eyes and pretend he was hugging me tight.

Other girls at school had posters of boy bands and movie stars on their bedroom walls. I had a framed class photo, and I kissed it every night. I'd pout my lips and hope they landed solely on Rennie and not either of the boys he stood between.

I didn't know how to be around him anymore. We'd gone from being thick as thieves to awkward and distant. That summer it was like someone had drawn an invisible line and stuck girls on one side, boys on the other, and it sucked. The girls were too mature for the boys, and the boys made the girls a target for their jokes and pranks.

That Halloween was the first one where we hadn't gone Trick or Treating together. I'd gone to Jenna Harper's house for a party, and the boys had run amok through the town, throwing eggs at shops and toilet paper over trees.

The next day, I turned up for my Saturday shift and found Rennie cleaning it all off before we even opened up. From inside, I'd stood the entire time watching him through the window with a cocked hip, crossed arms, and a scowl across my face like I already owned the place. But while my face was furious, something inside my body was going haywire.

His arms, his hands, the way his hoodie rode up and showed me the underwear that was always sitting above his jeans. He was the only one who cleaned up, and afterwards he came inside and apologised to both Gramps and me. He even bought me flowers. It was like he knew how much the place mattered to me too, and I had never felt more understood.

"I remember," he says.

"At first I thought it was just because you were scared, and I almost laughed at you, but then you didn't let go. And then you stroked my thumb with yours."

"Like this?" He interlaces his fingers with mine then sweeps his thumb, much bigger now, along the top of mine, almost to the tip and then back down again to a sensitive spot on my wrist.

"Yeah," my eyes fall shut. "Like that."

"And it felt good?"

"Uh huh."

"I wanted to kiss you that night," he says, his gentle strokes sending sparks all the way up my arm.

WHAT? I open my eyes and find him staring at our hands. "Why didn't you?"

"I thought you would laugh at me. Or worse, cry."

"I'd probably have cried with happiness," I confess.

"Really?" A wide smile spreads across his face, then he rolls his lips over his teeth to suppress it.

"Yeah, I went home and touched myself and pretended my hand was your hand."

His eyes fly to mine and his jaw drops. "Did you?" I nod and when he gives a little shake of disbelief, I can tell he's picturing it.

"I'm shocked. And here I always thought you were such a sweet girl." The stroking is firmer now, and all I can think about is that thumb teasing circles somewhere else.

"Sweet girls like orgasms too, you know." I can't believe I'm saying this to him.

"I figured that out when I found you listening to porn in your car."

"It was not porn! And I do not masturbate in the car. Well, not very often."

Rennie's future wife wouldn't talk about these things so directly, but right now a stupid part of me wants to shock him. Show him I'm not the sweet girl everyone thinks I am.

My thumb mirrors his movements and I feel like I'm in a regency romance, about to explode from the mere act of hand-holding.

Being here cooped up in his house is driving me sex crazy. I'm bored, and horny, and it's unbearable having him so close. The heat from his hand, the scent of his skin, the fire in his eyes. And still no release.

I've pushed it too far. Rennie clears his throat, places his hand on my thigh and he stands to leave. The sight of his big hand covering so much of my bare skin makes me whimper and slump further down on the sofa.

"What's wrong?" he asks in a panic. "Are you hurt?"

"Nothing, I'm just frustrated."

"I know, Bec, you'll be back on your feet soon enough."

"It's not that, I'm—" he hovers in the middle of the room.

"What?"

"I'm... I'm super horny OK?" Rennie stands there staring down at me and I, full of shame, look down at my feet. "I know, you're right, I am a filthbag but I haven't come in ages and orgasms are a form of stress relief, you know, and I can't do shit with my arm like this and I'm actually going insane."

When he doesn't say anything, I glance up at his face. I expect to see a look of shock, but he's biting his lip. His arms folded across his chest, he taps his fingers against his bicep.

"Don't laugh at me."

"I'm not laughing," he says. "I'm... processing."

I roll my eyes and pick up the remote to flick through channels, but he swipes it from my hand and hits the off button.

"Do you want me to help you? With this... problem." *He's surely not serious?*

"No, I could never ask that of you. I'm just venting, sorry."

His silence drags on and on. "You could ask."

"What?" I don't know what's more mortifying, this or the audiobook nightmare I still haven't managed to strike from memory.

"You could ask. Ask me."

I pull a blanket up over my face. "I think that's pushing our friendship a boundary too far, Renn."

"So push it." *Oh fuck, he is serious.* I can't even look at him.

"Bec," he says, his voice deeper as he leans over me and pulls the covers back. He rests his fists on either side of my hips and I stop breathing when he lowers his face unbearably close to mine. "Ask me to help you come."

Blood roars in my ears and I swear minutes pass before I finally get the courage to squeak out my words. "Could you help me come?"

Rennie closes his eyes and inhales deeply, a pause just long enough to make me regret this entire conversation. "Oh god, OK, you're playing with me. Don't worry, I'm being ridiculous. I'm an awful mess. I'm just frustrated and really I don't have much success with guys touching me anyway, so it's pointless."

He's still not moving. This is so embarrassing, and yet, unfathomably, I keep prattling on. "Forget I said anything. I'll survive. I've already survived a freak accident, how bad could a few days without an orgasm really be? I mean plenty of people go *years* and they're just fine, so... Jesus Rennie, are you going to talk soon or are you going to let me keep rambling all night?"

Rennie ducks his head into my chest and before I know it, I'm being lifted up and over his shoulder again. "Let's go."

11

Bec

Rennie's thick forearm wraps around the back of my thighs, holding me tight as he carries me past the spare bedroom, down the hallway, and into his.

This can't be happening.

I've never been in here before, though I've dreamed about it many times. I should be taking in every detail, but whatever is happening right now is not in this universe, and I can't concentrate on anything but his bed when he perches me on the end of it.

I don't know where to look while he adjusts the pillows into a pile. Opening his bedside drawer, he pulls out a small bottle and rests it on the nightstand. *What is that? Oh my god, is that lube?* Lube! Why does Rennie have lube, and who the *fuck* is he using it with?

He must see me staring and cuts my brain spiral off before I get even more enraged at the thought of him with anyone else. "Massage oil." *Ah. Ohhh.*

He settles himself in the middle of the bed, sitting up against the headboard. I just sit there, awkward as hell, while he parts his legs and pats the space in between them. I shimmy up until his hands grip my waist and pull my body into his.

"Lean against me," he says, and I do, wiggling a little to get comfy. I fold my arms across my stomach, tuck my knees up. I'm a bundle of nerves.

"You're wound up so tight, Bec." *You have no fucking idea, pal.* "Let me help you relax."

With one of those giant hands, he presses on the tops of my thighs until my legs stretch out in front of me.

"Your ankle OK?" he asks and I nod. He lifts my right arm, draping it gently over his thigh before doing the same on the other side. I'm in a vest top and pyjama shorts, my wrist and my foot still in supports but laying against him like this, I've never felt more naked.

"I'm sorry, Renn, this is the least attractive I've ever been."

"Shut your mouth." His firm tone is unexpected, but it scratches at a spot in my brain that has heat pooling in my belly in an instant. Careful not to press against my neck brace, he adjusts my head so it's nestled into his shoulder.

"You comfy?" he asks.

"Yes."

"You in pain?"

"Agony," I laugh nervously, and I'm grateful that he laughs with me. *What the hell are we doing?* He slides his hands up my forearms all the way to my shoulders, his thumbs coasting back and forth.

"Shall we take this off?" he reaches for the clasp at the back of my neck brace. "Just for a little while."

It's only been a day but I feel exposed without it, like my skin can't handle the contact with air. With one hand on my forehead, he settles me back against him, then slips his finger underneath the strap of my top and peels it off my shoulder. He reaches for the oil, drizzles a little in his palm and rubs them together right in front of my face. I swear my tongue hangs out of my slack jaw when his fingers slip back and forth between each other. New kink unlocked. I'll be looking at hand porn for weeks.

Being in Rennie's arms like this is a full sensory experience, and I notice everything. The featherlight stroke of his fingertips over my shoulder, the goosebumps they leave in their wake. The heat of his breath against my cheek. The scent of him this close, I get the layer beneath the smoke too, the base note of him. The sight of his thick, muscular thighs penning me in. I just wish I could taste him to complete the set. I want to lick him, bite him, swallow him down.

"You have a bruise," he says softly as he strokes up and down the side of my neck.

"From the seatbelt," I say, as if he won't know. He spreads the oil out to my shoulders and back again, sliding a little higher each time.

"Is this pressure OK?"

"Uh huh," I choke out. It's more than OK, this is the best thing that's ever happened in my entire life. It feels so good. Good because it's hitting a knot I hadn't realised was there. Good because I'm relaxing more by the second. Good because it's him and he's touching me. I float my eyes closed and let him take over, but still I can't escape my thoughts. I wonder how he's so good at this, who else he touches.

"Renn," I whisper. "Are you seeing anyone?" I hadn't asked him back the other day, and I don't know why, but it suddenly feels important to know.

"No," he says with a firm squeeze of my shoulders. "I'm not seeing anyone."

It makes absolutely no sense to me. "Why are you single?"

"Why are you?"

"I asked first."

"I guess I haven't found anyone quite right for me yet." It feels vulnerable to hear, and I'm glad I can't see his face, and that he can't see mine.

"What do you mean? There's a woman around every corner ready to jump your bones."

He laughs softly and his breath against my shoulder sends goosebumps in every direction. "None of them are quite... compatible."

"What does compatible mean?"

He takes a deep breath. "The things I'm looking for would have most women running a mile." *Jesus.* Why does he sound like a serial killer, and why is it so hot? I swear romance novels have rewired my brain.

"Like what?" I press. His slow exhale ghosts past my ear, setting my cheek on fire. His mouth is so close to my skin.

"I need someone who's not afraid to push things a little. To be pushed."

"In bed?"

"Yeah. I'm not exactly a vanilla guy."

Oh my god. Alistair Rendall? Surely not. The gentleman of all gentlemen has a dark side.

"You want someone who's not afraid to get a little rough?" I've read every kind of smutty book going, concocted a million fantasies, and I've never been more turned on than I am from just a shoulder rub and a handful of suggestive sentences.

"Exactly," he says, his voice low, almost taunting. "I don't think there's anyone in this town like me." How have I not known this about him? Has someone who can give me what I need been in front of me this whole time? *Could he? Would he? There's only one way to find out.*

"Rennie..." I close my eyes and hope I won't regret this. "I think I'm like you. And I'm not afraid to be pushed."

12

Rennie

Jesus, fuck. How is this happening? One minute we're watching TV, then she's asking me to get her off. Now she's telling me she's not afraid of getting a little rough?

My head and my dick are raging against each other. My head says I've pushed her into this. I could tell she was frustrated about something, I just didn't expect it to be that. My dick says, *God, I love touching her.* My head tells me I'm taking advantage of her situation, but this is Bec, I've always tried to do what's right by her. My dick says, *What's an orgasm between friends in her hour of need?* My gut says I'm far too eager to take this further.

I don't even know if she's saying what I think she's saying. Is she asking me to be rough with her? I've never really spoken about this stuff with anyone before, and even now we're dancing around it. I've spent my life pushing those desires deep down. I know you're not supposed to want to touch women this way.

"Renn?" *Shit, I didn't realise I'd stopped moving.* "You OK?"

"Are you?" *I can't move.*

"I'm good. That feels great. Keep going." *OK, I can do this.*

I run my hands back up to her shoulder and with one keeping her in place, I coast the other down over her chest. From this angle, I'm blessed with the beautiful view of the rise and fall of her breasts under my hand. Her white vest has ridden up a little, exposing a sliver of tender flesh above the waistband of her pyjama shorts. I want to taste it, bite it, mark it, make it mine.

I focus on the shift in her breathing when I stroke my fingers across the bare skin there. I've thought about this thousands of times, but never imagined she would feel so good. I force myself to concentrate on the massage, rubbing the rest of the oil into her soft skin. I know she's horny and frustrated, she said so herself, but I feel paralysed. I said I would help, but I have no idea where to go from here.

As if she can read my thoughts, she says, "Renn, touch me more."

I grip the hem of her top in my fist and pause. I should end this. This is a dangerous game to play with her, and if I start, I might not be able to stop. But it's too late, I've already got her in my arms.

With every hour I've spent in her recent company, it's becoming increasingly apparent that I know nothing about Rebecca Charlton. I don't know where she goes or who she dates. I don't know what she likes and what gets her screaming, but I'm dying to find out. If she wants my help, then she's damn well going to get it. I drag the front of her vest up over her tits, and we both groan when they spring free.

I saw Bec topless once, years ago, when a bunch of us went to an old school friend's beach wedding and ended up skinny dipping after too many beers. I've held onto the memory of that night, the silhouette of her frame in the moonlight, the full curve of her breast, but this is something else. She arches her back, her nipples point skyward, and my dick rages behind her.

I hold the bunched fabric at her throat, careful not to add any pressure near her bruise, and reach the fingers of my other hand up to trace the edges of her pretty little mouth. She follows my lead, parting her lips and darting her tongue out to wet the tips of my fingers. It takes every ounce of control not to slip them further inside, to push her to the edge of her comfort.

Pulling them free, I lower my hand to run my slick fingertip gently around her nipple and watch it stiffen under my touch. I can't believe she's letting me do this.

"Yes," she hisses. When I glance back at her face, she has her eyes closed. I wonder where she goes in her head. I don't want her thinking of anyone else, so I pinch the other nipple hard and bring her focus back to me.

"Do you have a toy or something you want me to use?"

"You didn't pack it!" she smacks my thigh, playfully. "I just want you."

Fuck, that feels good to hear. I bring my hand to her mouth, and I'm firmer this time, pushing two fingers between her lips, reaching for the back of her tongue. She closes firmly around them and I feel her lapping at me, sucking them deeper into her mouth. Hell, if this is what she's like with my hand, I can't imagine how she'd feel if she blew me.

No, I literally *can't* imagine it, because if I think about it for more than a second, I'm gonna come in my underwear. I pull my fingers from her mouth, and push my hand straight into the front of those tiny fucking shorts, wet fingers seeking her heat.

The sound of her whimpering has me throbbing against her back as she squirms under my touch. She must feel how much of an effect this is having on me.

"This what you need?"

"God yes."

She's already soaked. I force myself to focus on slow, rhythmic strokes, exploring her with no sudden movements that might aggravate her injuries. Bec might be challenging everything I ever thought I knew about her, but she's still this precious thing. I have to keep her safe in my arms. Her body tenses when my fingertips home in on her clit and start working her in soft, lazy circles.

"Can you come like this?" I want to make her feel as good as she feels when she's on her own, to touch her as well as she touches herself.

"Yeah... no... oh god Renn, I need more."

"Tell me what you need."

"I need your dick." *Jesus, I never knew she had a mouth like that.*

"You'd like that, wouldn't you?" I whisper into her ear. *God knows I'd like that too.* "I like hearing you beg for my dick, but not today."

"Renn, you don't have to be gentle with me. Please don't hold back. I want you to fuck me."

"You're lucky you're injured, or you might regret saying that."

I hook my thumbs into the waistband of her shorts. When I shove them down over her hips, she shimmies to help me get them free, but it makes her vest fall back in place, and I miss her nipples instantly.

"Open your mouth." I bunch the soft material together and pull it up. With one hand on either side of her head, I pull it into her mouth and set it between her teeth, gagging her. "Bite down."

She moans when she does it and I see her eyes flutter closed.

"Good girl. Don't let go." She moans again and her hips roll all by themselves, desperately seeking contact, anything. Damn, my girl likes to be praised. I love that. More than anything else, learning how her body reacts to me is getting me so fucking hard.

I cup her firmly between the legs with my palm, tease her with a few strokes and then slip a finger inside her, a decade of dreams coming true. She tips her head forward to watch me add another.

"Don't strain your neck."

"I want to see," I think she says through her makeshift gag. *Fucking hell.*

"You've thought about this before?"

She answers with a nod, and I tease them in and out of her in slow, firm strokes. It isn't long before I see the telltale shake of her thighs, feel her tighten around me, but this is way too soon. I make her come and this is all over. I'm not ready to deal with the aftermath.

I take my hand away and she cries out. "More," she pleads and who am I to deny her everything she wants? I push them back in, harder this time, and reach down with my other hand to rub her swollen clit. Her hips lift from the bed and I press my wrists down to keep her pinned in place. Her hands fly up to my biceps and grip them hard, but I pull my hand away and settle her sprained wrist back at her side.

"Don't move. Rest, baby."

She moans and writhes some more. This is what I love. To be in control, to build her up, to have her aching and needy for my touch.

"Wait!" she calls out, the nails of her good hand digging into my arm. I like that feeling way too much but I take my hands off her in an instant. If she doesn't want this, I don't either.

"What's wrong?"

"This is going too fast, I need a second. I need to commit it all to memory." *Well that's fucking adorable.*

"You're cute," I laugh, "but trust me, you won't forget this. Did I say you could open your mouth?"

I wrap my fingers underneath her thigh, hitching it further up mine then give her a sharp slap between the legs that has her buckling and yelping against me. For a second I panic I've gone too far.

"Again," she begs.

Fuck, yes. "Oh, you filthy girl. You like it when I own you?"

"Yes Renn, yes." Another smack, quickly followed by a third, has her mewling in my arms. This is what I want, what I have always craved. This primal urge to please her body over and over, to make her mine, to break her down until she's a shaking wreck that only I can put back together again.

Two fingers stroke the most hidden parts of her while her clit gets the full attention from my other hand. I don't even know how long it's been since I last slept with someone, but I've never touched anyone like this. Getting to watch her from this angle, seeing how her body reacts to my touch, it's everything. Bec in my arms, in my bed, is a gift I never thought I'd get. I drop my head to her neck and - *fuck* - she smells incredible. Her skin, her hair, her desire mixed with my shower gel is intoxicating.

I drag my tongue over her roughly and take her delicate flesh between my teeth. I want to bite her so hard I leave teeth marks, but I don't want to scare her. This is not about me or my depraved urges.

I'm about to let go, I need to give her nipples a little more attention, when her moans deepen. She rolls her hips faster and I let her fuck my hand, loving the way she grinds back against the length of me when she pushes and pulls. My dick is rock hard and I wonder if she can feel what she's doing to me, or if she's too caught up in her own sensations. I hope so, this is all for her.

I wasn't lying. She's lucky she is injured, and in a way I'm lucky too because I'm forced to hold back. This need I have to possess her, it's building in my chest. Using my hands to get her off like this barely scratches the surface of the things I'd do if I let that dark part of me out of its cage. I'm on the cusp of unleashing something I've buried for a long time.

I push it away and concentrate on her body, on building her up to exactly where I want her. My fingers press harder, my strokes become more focused, the wet sound of her pleasure filling the room. My other hand finds the pulse in her throat, and I get a sick thrill knowing I've made it race like a trapped animal. I feel her throb under my fingers and watch her chest rise and fall until her stomach tightens, shoulders turning inward. Her body clenches around me, her breath comes short and fast, until she's crying out, her orgasm rushing through her. Bec turns her face into my neck, squeezing her eyes shut until the feeling crests and subsides. She relaxes against me, but I don't stop, my hand massaging, spreading her wetness between her legs. I can't stop. I've got her in my arms now and I don't ever want this to end. Her coming in my hand like that is somehow both the hottest thing I've ever seen and not nearly enough.

This is why I've never made a move. It will never be enough. *She'll* never be enough to satisfy the beast inside me.

"Oh Renn, oh god. Nobody has ever... please... I can't—" Her thighs squeeze together, she says she can't take any more, and something in me snaps. I'm not having it for one second. Every ounce of restraint disappears. I hook my ankles over the top of her knees, pulling her legs wide apart, and she gasps at the force of it.

"Do you think we're done here, Bec?" Her perfect body tenses in my arms and I pull my hands away, reaching up to squeeze her tits, to fill her mouth with my drenched fingers. "I've waited my whole life to get my hands on you. You think I'm gonna let you stop at one orgasm?"

"Oh god, oh god," she garbles around my fingers, but there's no mistaking the way she laps them clean.

I press my mouth to her ear. "How often do you make yourself come?"

"Every day." Her chest heaves for air.

"Once a day, or more?"

When she doesn't answer, I pinch her nipple and tug hard. "How many times Bec?"

"Two or three!" she yelps. "Two or three."

I switch to a gentle caress. "See, all this time I thought you were a sweet girl and now I can't get that picture out of my mind. You getting yourself off all day long. Do you think about me when you do it?"

"Yes," she whimpers. *God, yes.* I'm gonna need to know every detail of every dirty fantasy she's ever dreamed up, but that will have to wait.

"Did you come on the morning of the accident?"

"No, there wasn't time."

"So that's... two days ago. Three orgasms a day. That's six you've missed out on." I take her earlobe between my teeth, "Let's catch you up."

I thrust my fingers back into her and pin her to my chest when she squirms in my arms.

"Oh God, Rennie, that's too much, I can't take it."

"I think you can," I growl.

13

Bec

I'm dead. I must have died in the car accident. That's the only explanation for everything that has happened in the past, however long Rennie has been doing this to me. What's worse is I don't even know if this is heaven or hell. How can something so good also be not nearly enough?

Rennie insists I can come again and, with his fingers hitting exactly the right spot, I do, more quickly than I'd ever manage on my own. My core tightens and I'm completely at his mercy. My orgasm rattles through me, every muscle tightens, and a sphere of white heat shoots through my veins. I squeeze my eyes shut, certain that if I open them, this dream will be over.

I'm floating out of my body, but then I realise it's Rennie lifting me, settling me down next to him, adjusting the pillows to support my neck. And then he's not touching me, and the absence of the heat of his body leaves me shivering.

"Tell me what you want." I hear his command, and when I dare to look, he's standing at the foot of the bed, an unmistakable bulge in his trousers that has me reaching for him.

I can't take anymore, but this is one blazing inferno that refuses to go out. "Please Renn, I need you."

"Say it again," he says, grabbing my hand and pinning it to my bare stomach.

"I need you inside me," I yell so loudly it makes him gasp, eyes wide. Shame heats my cheeks at my brazen request.

He lifts my good leg and kisses my ankle, nipping the tender skin between his teeth. "Listen to you, crying out for my cock. Do you think my neighbours can hear you begging? What will everyone say? Sweet little Rebecca Charlton laid out like this for me."

Who is this man? I've never seen him so possessive, so commanding, so *fucking male*. His words make me clench around nothing and groan at the torture of not having him already. I'm dying to feel him push into me, the stretch, the fullness I crave so much.

Kneeling on the bed, he works his way up my calf, nipping, and licking, and sucking until he reaches the top of my thigh. "God, you look incredible."

I always thought it was an exaggeration when one of my books described a woman as quivering with lust, but I get it now. I'm trembling *everywhere*. It's lust, and it's fear, this constant build-up and release and then blissful agony when he doesn't stop touching me.

And I hope he doesn't stop because I know the minute he does I'm going to have to face this. Face what we've done. *How will I ever look him in the eyes again?*

I'll deal with that later, right now I'm desperate to get my hands on him. I reach out for a handful of his hair, so much softer than I imagined, but he lifts my hand away and sets it down at my side.

"Don't move." I love his firm tone, the way he puts me in my place, but it also makes me want to push it, to push him and see how he'll react if I don't follow his orders. When he moves to plant kisses all over my stomach, I reach out again, spreading my fingers through his hair to drag my nails over his scalp. For a moment, he leans into it and a deep moan rumbles from his chest. I can tell he likes it, but in an instant he rises above me, grabbing my wrists and pinning my arms above my head.

"I'm sorry, I'm sorry," I yelp. "I can't help it. I need to touch you."

"Do your arms hurt like this?"

"No, I'm fine."

"No touching," he says, pointing his finger close to my face. I stick out my tongue and lap at the tip of it. He groans loudly and his face crumples until he regains his composure. "If you don't quit it, I'll have to tie you up."

"Oh god, yes please." I lift my hips to grind up against him, from this angle he seems even harder than before.

"Fucking hell," he says through gritted teeth. "Who are you?"

He moves back down the bed and I concentrate on staying still, readying myself for whatever comes next. I close my eyes, but Rennie has other ideas.

"Look at me, Bec," he barks, and when I open up, he's right there at my apex, dark heat in his eyes. "Do you know how long I've wanted to taste you?" *Oh Jesus.* I could come just from the way he speaks to me.

A long, slow sweep with his tongue sends my eyes rolling back in my head and then he pulls away again. "You look away and I'll stop Bec. Do you understand?"

I moan out a yes and blink hard, forcing my vision to focus on him. He hooks his arms underneath my thighs and grips onto my hips, holding me steady. The flat of his tongue drags through my centre, carving me open.

"Oh god, Bec," he moans, "you taste so fucking good."

Well, this is unexpected. Alistair Rendall talks dirty like the best book boyfriends. Unexpected and incredible.

With other guys this has always felt like a courtesy, a quick detour before the main event, but Rennie goes down on me like a man starved. Every stroke of his tongue shows me this is exactly where he wants to be. It's an exquisite mix of firm licks and fast flicks that have my mind spinning. I feel devoured and adored, and when he moans against me I can't tell which of us is enjoying it more.

He moves his mouth further north, pressing kisses around my clit while his fingers slip back inside me. "Does that feel good, baby? Is this what you need?"

I nod and let the wave of another orgasm begin to roll through me. His fingers and tongue are a combination I've only ever read about, and my god it is fucking heavenly. With every stroke, every lick, I feel that pressure building up inside me again, coaxing me closer to the edge.

I try to hold back, I never want this to end, but I'm not in charge here. Even with Rennie pinning me to the bed, I can't stay still. My hips rock against his touch, my back arches, my legs shake on either side of him.

At the last second, he pulls his hand away and clamps his mouth around me, sucking so hard I buck up off the bed. That only encourages him. He sucks more, a bruising kiss that pulls my orgasm, then my shattered soul, from deep within me. I cry out, and shoot forwards, curling into a ball around his head. I grab onto his hair, his shoulders, and Rennie, *this fucking man*, pushes his face harder against me and does *not. Stop. Sucking.*

"Too much, too much," I scream and finally, finally, he pulls his mouth away. I roll onto my side, every inch of me twitching, clenching, vibrating with pleasure. He climbs up the bed, settles himself behind me, and carefully moves me into a more comfortable position.

"Lie back, Bec. I can't have you thrashing around like that."

"Then don't give me more whiplash from coming," I manage to say through heavy panting.

He rests one big, warm hand on my stomach and strokes slowly back and forward with his thumb, the motion helping my breath fall back into a normal rhythm.

Rennie drops his lips to my shoulder and chuckles against my skin. "OK, I think we can save a few for another day." *What is he saying? Are we going to do this again? I bloody hope so.*

He pulls my top back down, covering my chest, then hooks the straps back up over my shoulders. "You stay right there."

I couldn't move even if I wanted to. I am a pile of mush. He returns a minute later, towering over me with a glass of water, my pain meds, and a warm washcloth. I take him in, tall, broad, still completely clothed. I feel like prey under his burning gaze. Inching myself up against the pillows, I drink down the water while he cleans me up. It's such an intimate gesture it makes me want to cry.

He must sense it. "Are you OK?"

"Yeah, that was... it was amazing. I've never—" I can't find the words.

"Oh, fuck." His jaw drops and he pulls away from me, panic in his eyes. "You're a virgin?"

"No," I laugh it off, but his reaction makes me uncomfortable. I mean, I know I haven't had sex in a long time, but does he really think I made it to my thirties without doing *anything*? As my body cools, reality hits. I'm half naked. In Rennie's bed. And he made me come. Multiple times.

In all my fantasies about him, I've never considered that the aftermath is far more vulnerable than the act itself. I cover my hands with my face until we both break the silence at the same time.

"I'm sorry, I didn't mean to imply—"

"I've just—"

"You go," he says.

"I've never done anything like that."

"What do you mean?"

"Nobody has ever made me come like that. You made it all about me."

"As it should be." He reaches out to tuck a loose strand of hair behind my ear. Oh now he's back to being a gentleman, and the guilt rolls in. I've not even made an attempt to satisfy him, and the tent in his trousers looks painful at this point.

"I, um, do you want me to..." I nod downwards, "you know, help you out?"

"No, you need to rest." He pulls the covers back, then reaches underneath me, lifting me gently to one side of the bed before covering me up. Walking around to the other side, he takes his clothes off and I try not to lose my mind at the sight of his gorgeous, naked arse right there in all its ripe, toned, biteable glory. To my great dismay, Rennie pulls on fresh underwear from his drawer then settles next to me on the bed but stays on top of the covers.

"Here, sit up," he says, lifting my neck brace off the nightstand.

"I'm not putting that stupid thing back on. It's revolting."

"Don't be so stubborn."

"I'm fine. If you can just fetch my crutches, I'll go."

"You sleep here."

I hadn't thought about it in the moment, but I'd assumed I'd go back to his spare room after we were done. Mission accomplished, help administered, absolutely ridiculous favour granted. Why would he still want me here?

Then I remember his words.

"All this time, I thought you were a sweet girl."

"I've waited my whole life to get my hands on you."

"Do you know how long I've wanted to taste you?"

I thought this was all about me. Rennie gave me exactly what I wanted, but could it be that I've given him something he's been craving too? Has he been thinking about me the way I've been thinking about him? And if he has, where do we go from here? Our friendship will never be the same again.

"Renn," I whisper.

"Yes, baby?" he says quietly, stroking my hair away from my face. His hair is all over the place, and I love knowing it was me who messed it up.

"I will never be able to look at you the same after this. And I can't believe you had the nerve to call me a filthbag."

He laughs softly, dreamily, and when he tips his forehead to rest against mine, I am completely, utterly gone.

14

Bec

Rennie has slept with one arm around my duvet-covered waist all night, the other tucked up underneath his pillow. I slept better than I have in ages, but I've been lying here for a while thinking about how to get up and pee without bursting this bubble.

I study his face, his long eyelashes. I hunt for the little scar above his eyebrow, a memento from when he ran into a goalpost in primary school. Stubble creeps in across his jaw, and I count the tiny lines on his full lips. He looks pretty damn cute when he's asleep. I take it all in while I have the chance.

This is the strangest feeling. Me being here, in Rennie's bed, cocooned in the covers while he's stayed on top of them all night. I don't know if that's for my benefit, a show of respect, or if he just doesn't want to be as close to me as I'd like. I wish he was under here with me so I could touch him, press my face into his chest, run my hands over his muscles, loop our legs together and grind myself against one of those delicious, firm thighs. All those orgasms he gave me last night have done nothing to slake my thirst for him. If anything, I want more, but all I have to go on are a few things said in the heat of the moment. I don't know what he wants at all.

I watch as his lips twitch and his brows knit together. I wonder if he's dreaming, and what about.

"No," he grunts in his sleep. His head moves back and forth, followed by more unintelligible grumbles. Eyes still closed, he tightens his grip and pulls me closer.

"Rennie," I whisper, not sure if he's still asleep. "Are you OK?"

His eyes squeeze together for a few seconds. "Bad dream," he says, blinking it away. I keep watching him as he crosses back into the land of the living. When his eyes open and meet mine, the sweetest smile spreads across his face.

"You're here," he moans, then breathes a sigh heavy with something like relief. I nod and smile when he lifts my arm and rests it gently above the waistband of his boxers. I flex my fingers. His skin is warm and smooth and I want to stroke it, but my bladder is screaming for my attention.

"I need the loo," I whisper.

"OK, do you need help?" he asks.

"No, I'll manage. Just keep your eyes closed, I'm only half dressed."

His warm hand finds me under the covers, smooths across my back, and down over my hips to give me a good squeeze. "Mmm, I love this bum."

I shimmy out of his arms and manage to sit up then reach down for the clothes he abandoned last night. I wriggle back into my pyjama shorts and glance over my shoulder to make sure he's not sneaking a peek, but of course he's not. Even after spending god knows how long with his hands on me last night, he's respectful.

"Hurry back," he mumbles, and my stomach flips.

I half hop, half hobble to the bathroom to freshen up. After a quick slug of mouthwash, I attempt to wrangle my hair back into a bun, but it keeps catching on this stupid wrist guard. I'm taking this off today, I'm sick of it. In the end, I just let my hair down and rake my fingers through it, hoping it doesn't look too wild.

I climb back into his bed, but a minute away from Rennie is all it took for the mist of doubt to descend. It feels needy to slide back into his arms, so I sit upright in the space next to him. I don't want to do this, the awkward morning after thing. What must he think of me, begging him to touch me like that? I know we can't avoid it, not while I'm stuck staying at his house.

Beside me, Rennie stretches out, arching his back and giving me a perfect view of his muscles springing into action. A smattering of hair covers his chest, trailing down the centre of his stomach and beyond.

I've snuck glances at topless Rennie when I've bumped into him at the pool, or when he's run past the shop on a hot day, his sweat-soaked t-shirt hanging from his back pocket, but I've never been treated to a private show like this.

The calendar the station crew made to raise funds for new playground equipment doesn't count. The whole thing was a big joke, but I can't pretend I wasn't pleased to discover that the black-and-white photo of Rennie standing under the spray of water in tiny, tight boxer shorts fell on my birthday month. Getting to stare at him for 31 days was the best gift I've ever received.

"How are you feeling?" he asks.

Ooft, what a question. "Um, awkward, embarrassed, mildly ashamed." *Good one, Bec, you could have just said "fine".*

"I meant physically."

Jesus christ. My libido sparks back to life, though I'm not sure it ever fully died down. How does he always set me on edge with so few words? "Oh, well, er, yeah, pretty good in that department."

He bites his lip to stifle his laugh. "I meant your wrist, your leg, your injuries." He rolls to face me, propping his head up on his hand and quirks one eyebrow. "Though I'm glad to hear you're satisfied."

Gah, so flirty I might die.

"Oh god," I pull the covers up and bury my face. "I'm not good at this."

"Good at what?"

"Pillow talk. Post match analysis. Whatever this is."

Rennie tugs the edge down to expose my eyes, my shame. "We don't have to talk about it if you don't want to." His fingers reach up, lifting a lock of hair from where it hangs over my forehead. My eyes follow his as he watches it twist around his finger before he tucks it behind my ear. I'm speechless under his gaze. To have him this close, touching me, after what we did last night? I'm barely convinced it's real.

"Well, I'm starving," he says, bouncing upright with far more energy that I could muster. "Someone distracted me and I didn't even eat dinner last night."

"Oh god, I'm so sorry, I didn't mean for—"

"Shhh, I'm teasing you." Rennie presses a kiss to my forehead. *What is it with this man and these chaste kisses?* "You stay right here. I'll be back with breakfast."

From through the house, I hear him turn on the radio and start singing away to himself. I don't think I've ever heard Rennie sing before and I don't know why, he has a beautiful voice.

He returns with a tray, still only wearing his snug boxers. I can't look at him, but I can't look away, so I just sit there unable to speak, blood thumping through my veins.

"Scoot up," he says, and I follow his orders so he can set the tray on my lap. "Tea, toast, bit of fruit to get you going for the day."

While I nibble on toast, perfectly buttered, good man, I watch Rennie pull on a fresh t-shirt and trousers. I'm quite pleased to see several pairs hanging in his wardrobe, just as I suspected. He slips on a hoodie, adjusting the strings and... wait, where is he going?

"I have to run Mary to a doctor's appointment this morning," he says, reading my mind. "I have self-defence class at 6, then I'm on a late shift. I'll need to sleep a bit this afternoon, but can we hang out between then?" *He's going to leave me here? In his bed?*

"Mmm-hmm." I nod and stare into my tea. This cannot be real. Rennie and I are making plans for our day like it's the most normal thing in the world. Him doing all the things he did to me last night is one thing, one thing that admittedly I am still not quite processing, but he and I playing house is another entirely. What is he doing? What are *we* doing? My head is spinning.

"OK, spill it," he says.

"What?"

"Whatever you're thinking, just say it." He perches next to me on the edge of the bed, the length of his thigh pressed against mine. Once again, I find myself hating this stupid duvet that's always seems to be between us.

"I was just thinking about last night, and how you said..." *Oh god, this is horrible.* "You'd said you'd waited a long time for this."

"I did."

"Did you mean it? I mean, it's OK if you didn't. We all say things in the heat of the moment."

"What makes you think I didn't mean it?" he smiles and does that dreamy thing with his eyebrow again.

"Oh. Um. Well, I suppose I had no idea you felt that way."

"I guess you're not the only one good at keeping parts of themselves hidden."

And here was me thinking I knew this man. "Why have you never said anything?"

He lets out a long, slow breath. "I really respect you, Bec."

"You didn't seem all that respectful last night," I blurt out and Rennie's face crumples. His face crumples, and I know I've said the wrong thing. "I mean. You were respectfully disrespectful. In a good way."

He sinks his head into his hands and rubs at the back of his neck. Well done Bec, consider the bubble well and truly burst.

"OK, I'm going to stop talking. Thank you for last night, I'm going to go back to my room. Your room. The spare room." *Seriously Bec, stop talking.*

I set the tea down and try to get up, but Rennie stops me. With his hand splayed across my shoulder, he presses me into the pillows at my back.

"You are not to leave this bed until I get home, and then if you need any more help managing your orgasm addiction, I'm the man for the job." My eyes widen and my good hand flies to my mouth.

"Did you just squeak?" he asks and I nod, because that's the only way to describe the noise that came out of my mouth just then. His words turn me into such a mess. "That's fucking cute."

"So you would... you want to do this again?" My voice is small and hidden behind where I nibble my thumb. Rennie pulls it from my mouth and laughs. I'm confused. "What's so funny?"

His own thumb sweeps painfully slowly across my lips. "You have no idea how many things I want to do to you."

My gasp fills the space between us. "To me?"

"Do you see anyone else around here?" he says. I open my mouth, take the tip of his thumb between my teeth, and shake my head. His eyes flare and I can't help but close my mouth around him, darting my tongue out for the tiniest taste. A groan rumbles from his chest and sends a shock of heat through me. "So many things, Bec. To you. With you. On you. Underneath you." He peppers each statement with a kiss on my shoulder. I let go of his thumb as my head falls back against the pillow, desire rolling up my spine.

"You can't say things like that to me."

"Why not?"

"Because it's like a fantasy come true, and it's making me feel nuts."

He links his fingers with mine, gently flexing my wrist back and forth. "You have fantasies about me?"

"Come on," I poke him in the chest, "look at you, you must know how every woman round here feels about you."

"I don't care how other women feel. I'm asking what you think."

Welp. "Then yes, if it pleases you to know, I have thought about you that way."

"Tell me," he growls.

"No chance. Far too embarrassing. And anyway, too many. You'll be late for Mary."

"Write me a list." Rennie pulls open his bedside drawer and rifles for a notepad and pen.

"A list?" *Is he joking?*

"A list."

"Why?"

"Because it will give you something to do," he laughs. "And because that's my fantasy."

"What do you mean?"

"That's my fantasy," he presses his finger to the paper. "I find a list you've written of everything you want, and I make it my job to ensure you get it."

A list. A sexy wishlist? *This goddamn man.* I am the luckiest woman alive. And if the things I want don't push him away, I am about to get even luckier.

15

Rennie

I should have known this would happen. The drive from Mary's house to the doctor's surgery takes less than ten minutes, but every one of those minutes has so far been filled with her running her mouth about Bec. She's a tiny thing in the seat next to me, hands clasped over the handbag on her lap, but she can talk for England.

"The poor woman, Alistair. Now, if only she had a husband to take care of her, this might never have happened, you know."

"How do you figure that?"

"Well, she shouldn't have been out driving that old car in such atrocious weather. What was she even doing out there?"

"That's what I said!" I want to shout, but I stop myself. Bec doesn't need me and the nosy neighbours ganging up on her.

In all honesty, I can't allow myself to think about it too much. The vision of her car crushed underneath that tree is not something I'll ever forget, and every time that image flashes through my mind I find it hard to breathe. I need to get that under control.

"She was doing her job. The wedding catering, remember?"

"Well, if she had a husband, she wouldn't have to work," Mary scoffs. Ha! I'd like to see the fate of a man who would dare try to stop Bec from working. I can't imagine he'd last long.

"Come on now, Mary, the shop is her life. She'd hardly give it up just for some man."

"And why haven't you got a wife yet, Alistair? A whole gaggle of babies. That's what you need."

"Mary." My voice is a warning. Everyone thinks they know what I need and they hardly know me at all.

"Do you prefer men?" she says, a million miles off base. "It's OK if you do. Men can have children too, now you know. I read an article about it, so many ways. Modern technology is really something, eh?"

I shake my head and pull into the last space in the surgery's tiny car park. I climb out and walk round to open Mary's door and help her out.

"I do wish Rebecca had a husband, though. Someone to look after her properly." *And we're back to square one.* "You need to help her get back on her feet and find someone. Have you got any nice single friends at the station?"

Message received loud and clear. Everyone thinks Bec needs a husband. They just don't think it should be me.

And they're right. She deserves a good man. A safe, reliable man. Not some idiot who puts out fires for a living. Who wants to be far from gentle with her body. The thought of hurting her, or her worrying about me day and night is unbearable.

I picture her right now, there in my home. In my room. In my bed. I imagine her hair spread out on my pillow, infusing it with her scent. I think about the way she looked last night, nestled between my legs, coming apart under my touch. The way she moans, how soft and silky her skin is, how her body is everything I dreamed of and so much more. Knowing she's still there in my bed is torture when I'm here in this dusty old waiting room that has barely changed since I was a boy.

There's still an enormous fish tank in the corner, and one of those play tables where you push wooden shapes along the spiral and zigzag wires. I used to love that thing. Loved the feeling of taking the chaos someone had left behind and putting it back in order. That feeling of making it to the end, having all my beads lined up together in a neat row, nothing could beat it. That's a core memory right there.

I take a seat while Mary goes in for her appointment and pass the time staring at the noticeboard covered in faded posters. Stop smoking classes. Free diabetes check. Pregnancy yoga. Physiotherapy.

That reminds me, I need to check Bec has had a referral for physio. We should start exercises in a few days to help her build her strength back up. And not the kind of exercise we got up to last night.

There can't be any more of that. Jesus, what the hell was I thinking? Putting my hands on her the day after she nearly died. She's a guest in my home, there to recover, not for me to take advantage of and unleash my selfish ass upon. But then what are these fantasies she says she has?

I can't get my head straight. Can't see through the blurred lines of the Bec I've known my whole life, the Bec of my darkest desires, and the Bec who was spread out on my bed last night, clawing at my thighs as she thrust against my hand and moaned my name. Can it really be that all those versions of her are one and the same?

It doesn't matter anyway. She'll be better in a couple of weeks and then she'll go home, and that will be it. Helping Bec get what she needs is one thing. Letting myself loose on her precious, perfect body is not an option. Absolutely not. If I just keep telling myself this is all for her, then maybe I'll get through this in one piece. Then I'll have whatever the fuck this is out of my system, and Bec can move on with her life.

The house is quiet when I get home. Obviously, I've been hoping that she followed orders and she's still in my bed, but Bec's not one for being told what to do. I figured she'd be up watching TV, but there's no sign of her in the living room. Clean dishes on the drying rack tell me she must have gotten up after breakfast, so we'll have to have words about her not doing that again.

I walk down the hallway to the spare room, thrilled to find she's not in there either. There's only one place she could be and, *fuck*, this is too close to a fantasy I've had for years. One where I come home and find her waiting for me. I open the door to discover her kneeling on my bed wearing nothing but a blindfold and a smile. It's my birthday, and she's my gift.

Submissive and compliant, she's utterly gorgeous with her hair hanging down her smooth, pale back. I spend a long time staring at her before I dare touch her, taking in the slope of her neck, circling the bed to stroke down the base of her spine to where it curves into that perfect peach. In my fantasy she doesn't speak, so neither do I. Instead, I tell her everything I want to say with my hands, and my mouth, and my dick until we fill the silence with our moaning. My blood rushes south at the thought of it. This cannot be happening. She couldn't possibly know this shit I imagine about her.

I push the door ajar slowly and what I find is... well, what I find is not exactly what I had in mind. Still, it's so fucking cute I can't complain.

Bec is asleep, spread out like a starfish in the middle of my bed. Her limbs, hair, and blankets are all over the place. She's beautiful and chaotic and, judging by the drool pooling at the corner of her mouth, completely out of it. I spot her painkillers next to an empty glass on my nightstand with a pang in my chest.

She's still in pain. Still in her own personal hell. She needs rest and recovery far more than she needs me leering over her like a creep. I bury my fantasy down deep, where it belongs and where it must stay.

It's too early for me to try to sleep, but there's nowhere I want to be more than right here. I strip to my boxers and leave my clothes on the floor, slipping under the covers in next to her. This is what I wanted last night, but I also wanted her to feel safe. Not like I was going to maul her all night, even if that's all my dick wanted to do.

I lift her leg and roll her to her side to make space for me. I'm not used to sharing my bed. Having so much room to stretch out is probably the only perk of being single, but with her, I'd happily never sleep alone again.

"Hmm," Bec mumbles, all sleepy and soft, but then her head jerks back and forth. "No," she whimpers, stuck somewhere in her head that I can't get to. "No needles. Help me. Help me."

"Hey, shhh," I whisper, "it's OK. You're OK."

I curl my body around hers and scoot in a little further at the exact moment she scoots back. Her body is snug against my chest, her full, round ass pressed against my groin. I'm never getting to sleep like this.

When she snuggles in further, grinding a little, I'm not even sure she realises what she's doing. I should not be taking advantage of her in this state.

I put a little distance between us and she whimpers, reaching back to pull my arm around her waist. My hand settles where her t-shirt has ridden up a little. "Better," she moans.

I can't help myself, I splay my fingers and hold my breath when my thumb ghosts the underside of her breast. That soft, pale, bare flesh I'm desperate to taste. I want to squeeze and suck and nip it between my teeth. I know it's fucked up and possessive, but I want to leave bite marks. It's this awful need to control and own her.

It blows my mind to have my hands on her. Years of want and need and agony and now she's here in my bed it's... I honestly don't know.

My alarm goes off, and I'm alone, as usual. My blackout curtains are drawn, and with the door closed, it could be the middle of the night. It took a long time to get used to cramming sleep before a night shift. My body clock is off, my mind senses something's not right, and panic fills my chest.

I rub my eyes and I'm back in that road, scrambling to pull branches from the wreck of her car. Rough bark slices into my hands, but I don't care. The neanderthal storm whips up fast.

Bec was here.

Bec is missing.

Where is Bec?

Find Bec.

I leap out of bed, throwing the door open as I rush down the hallway, calling her name.

"I'm here," she calls back from the kitchen.

She's here, oh thank fuck. "What are you doing up?" I bark at her, fist rubbing away the pain behind my sternum.

"Not all of us are on a night shift. I'm guessing you *didn't* sleep well?"

"You're supposed to be resting. Not..." What *is* she doing? "Are you cooking?"

"Just some sandwiches Sarah dropped off. I thought you'd need the energy for beating up the kids."

"That's the exact opposite of self-defence classes." I scoop her up from behind and carry her through to the sofa. "You sit your ass down."

"Rennie stop," she bats at my arm wrapped around her waist. "I'm honestly fine. I can almost put weight on my ankle without the crutches now." She tries to get up and show me, but I push her back, lifting her leg to rest on the footstool.

"Almost isn't good enough. You heard the doctor. If you push it, you'll take longer to recover."

"OK, jeez, calm down. I was just trying to help."

"I'm supposed to take care of you, remember?" I say, pointing my finger close to her face. "Not the other way around."

16

Bec

Wow, Rennie in brute mode sure is something to behold. I don't know whether to be afraid or turned on. I mean, obviously it's the latter because Rennie looks the way he looks and I'm not afraid to indulge in a sexy grump fantasy from time to time. He huffs like a bull and storms off, back to where I've left our sandwiches toasting under the grill. I cross my arms, stick out my tongue, and sulk back.

"I can't just sit around and do nothing. I'll go insane."

"So go insane," he booms from across the breakfast bar.

"Why are you being so mean to me?"

"I woke up, and you weren't there. I thought you were gone."

This idiot. "Where would I go? I can't walk properly, I have no car. Oh god," I throw my hands up, "that reminds me I still need to call the insurance people. But that doesn't explain why you're acting like a bear with a sore paw because I left the room for four minutes."

"I am not." *Oh shit.* I see what's going on here. Rennie woke up, I was gone, and he freaked out.

"Ohhh, I get it. You missed me."

"No," he grunts.

"Rennie," I tease, drawing his name out. "Why are you freaking out on me?"

"I'm not," he says, but he refuses to look at me while he plates up our food. I study his face while he brings everything through. His jaw is set firm, but I see that telltale tick.

"OK, maybe I am freaking out a little bit. Look, I just—"

"What's going on?"

He lets out a slow sigh. "I've never done anything like what we did last night, either. That's not a thing I do with lots of people."

I gasp out loud and throw my hand to my face in mock horror. "You're a virgin!?"

"No," he chuckles softly, "and I'm sorry implied that you were. I just never see you with anyone."

Ugh, this is *not* a conversation I want to have with him. "Yeah, I don't date."

"Why not?"

"There's nobody in this town that I want to date." *Except you.* "You're one to talk. I never see you with anyone either. And what do you mean you've never done anything like last night?"

He tips his head back, considering his words while he finishes his mouthful of food. "I like to be in control, and it felt good that you let me do that." *Ooft. So hot.*

"I don't feel like I had much choice," I tease, taking a bite of my sandwich.

"What?" he says, horrified.

"No, I mean, I liked it. I liked that you took charge. That's what I like."

"Stop talking and eat your food."

The hour before Rennie leaves for his class is awkward as hell. He barely speaks more than two or three words at a time. He shuffles around the house, moving things around with no real purpose. Neither of us mention last night again, and while I watch a film with my ankle propped up, he sits on a stool by the breakfast bar, far from my reach.

I don't get it. Things seemed good when he left this morning, and I didn't exactly hate snuggling up with him when he came back to bed. How did we go from him promising me orgasms last night, demanding sexy wishlists this morning, to acting like an old married couple who can't stand to be around each other?

"What will you do with your evening?" he asks, lacing up his black leather boots.

"Rest, I suppose."

"Correct answer."

"Oh, you mean you don't have the Bridge club coming over to keep me company? There's no personal chef arranged for this evening?" His stupid, snarky mood is rubbing off on me.

"Do you need some company?" he asks, his voice a little softer.

"No Renn, I'm joking. I'd rather have some time to myself, so I'll just shut out the lights and read a book in bed." Of course I don't tell him it will be a dirty book and I'll be thinking of him the whole time. I pick up my phone to choose a new one to download.

"My bed," he says. His voice is closer, and when I look up, he's towering over me.

"What?"

I freeze when Rennie reaches out, ever so slowly, and strokes his fingers softly across my cheek. At my jaw they coast down my neck, leaving a trail of goosebumps in their wake. "Stay in my bed. Wait for me to get home."

"Your bed?" I can barely get the words out when he travels along my collarbone and up to my chin, caressing it as he tilts my face skyward.

"The mattress is better."

"Oh *sure*, the mattress is better." He slides his fingers higher, squeezing my mouth into a little pout, then blows a kiss into the air between us.

"I'll see you in the morning."

And then he's gone.

I sit, staring into the room, wondering what the hell is going on in this man's head? He's hot, then cold, then cute and while I don't hate riding Rollercoaster Rennie, I'm definitely starting to get emotional whiplash.

My fingers find their way to my lips, sure I can feel the imprint of his kiss. I'm ridiculous. He hasn't even kissed me. Not last night, not this morning, and not right now. My mouth is tingling like he has, though. Like he finally found his way to me, our lips connecting just as I've always dreamed they would. But here in the real world, the fact remains that Alistair Rendall has made me come - *multiple times* - but he still hasn't kissed me.

Although... that's not technically true. Rennie and I have shared precisely one kiss, forever and ever ago, and it didn't really count. I doubt he even remembers. It was a kiss between kids high on hormones, pilfered vodka, and end of school spirits. It was a good kiss, one that I thought about for weeks, but far too short. There was only the slightest bit of tongue, yet I felt seared. I threw up shortly afterwards, but let the record show that it had absolutely nothing to do with the kiss.

The kiss was perfect.

It was everything.

And then Jamie Parker took me home.

Jamie had moved in next door to me a few summers before with his mum and his stepdad. At school we'd been in different classes, and at weekends he stayed with his dad, so although I knew him, I didn't really *know* him.

Needless to say, waking up to find him asleep on the floor next to my bed was unexpected. While I dry-heaved into the bin, he rubbed my back and filled in the blanks from the night before.

Rennie and I kissing (that part I remembered), then me throwing up, Rennie leaving, me crying, me trying to hitch a ride home from a track in the woods where no cars ever drove, all ending with Jamie walking me home. He'd done the decent thing and, crucially, got me to bed without my parents realising what a state I was in.

When I noticed I was still wearing all of my clothes from the night before, I came to see Jamie in a whole new light. He was kind, he was caring, and he was also pretty cute.

Rennie and I barely saw each other that summer. I spent my days working in the shop, and Jamie would drive over to give me a lift home because he had a car, and so he could.

Summer turned into autumn, then winter, then spring. Before I knew it, Jamie and I had been dating for a year. Not that we'd ever put a label or anything on it, but that's what relationships are like when you're 19. We'd meet up after work, drive to the nearest multiplex to see a film, or sneak in and out of each other's bedrooms. I still don't know why we were always so secretive about being together. Most of the time I would just hang out while he played video games.

Sometimes on the 30 second walk from Jamie's back to mine, I'd spot Rennie and Sophie kissing on his doorstep. I don't know how it had come about, but he was happy, I was happy, and that's all that mattered. I wrote our kiss off as a drunken mistake, and I'm sure he never even thought about it.

17

Bec

Rennie arrives home from his night shift not long after I wake up from a long, but restless sleep. While he takes a second shower, I sit up and prepare myself for the conversation I've been mulling over since he left last night. I don't like how we left things, and I want to clear the air before I get up for the day.

I know he's stubborn about me taking it easy, but I'm honestly feeling OK. I'm capable of doing some things for myself, if not everything quite yet. I want my laptop so I can work, plus, I still need to talk about what happened the other night. My head is all over the place. The longer we don't address it, the more awkward I feel. Every time I woke up through the night, he was the first thing on my mind.

I slept in his bed, just like he told me to, but it wasn't the same without him there, and I made things worse by sniffing his pillow like a total sex creep. It was impossible not to long for his touch, so I channeled my sexual frustration into writing his list.

It wasn't exactly a hard task. I've always had a list of fantasies in my head, but it did little to settle down my rampant horn. Unfortunately, after filling out two pages - *I think I was very restrained* - my wrist really was aching too much for me to do much about it.

In the cold light of day, though, this whole list thing feels awkward as hell. I can't possibly give it to him. This whole situation is nuts.

What happens when this little holiday from reality ends? It has to end, right?

All rational thought flies right out of my head when he comes back to his room, rubbing his hair with a towel, wearing nothing but tight black boxers. This is fast becoming my favourite sight. The curve of his pecs, his broad chest tapering down into that solid v shape that I've spent far too long obsessing over.

Just like yesterday, he crawls into bed and, without a word, pulls me down into his arms, into the curve of his warm body. The clean scent of his shampoo fills my nostrils and makes me light-headed. One hand rests on my stomach. The other tracks a line down my spine before pulling me tighter.

His warmth makes me feel like I'm slipping under water. Everything else melts away. I'm floating beneath his touch, pressing against him. My back to his chest, my ass to his groin, my thighs to his thighs. He shifts down a little, his mouth pressing firm kisses to the side of my neck.

"I need you," he whispers into my ear. When his fingertips dance underneath the hem of my t-shirt, I lose the ability to breathe. "Need to touch you."

I don't know if it's a question, but my answer is a moan, a roll of my hips, a tilt of the head exposing more of my neck to him. I feel his lips ghost the shell of my ear, and the heat of his breath makes my eyes flutter closed.

"Can I make you come again?" he asks, his voice pleading like this is all for him. I nod and whimper out a yes when his hand pushes into my underwear. I'm under his spell. Couldn't stop him if I wanted to, which I absolutely do not.

His other arm slips underneath me, then up under the front of my t-shirt until he cups my breast in his hand and squeezes. It's the perfect pressure, firm and greedy.

"Fuck," he moans and I moan with him. "You feel so fucking good."

Between my legs, his touch is languid and sensual. "God, you're so wet. Is this for me?"

"Yes," I hiss. Rennie spreads his fingers around, the slick sensation against swollen flesh driving me further back against him.

Pulling out from underneath me, his other fingers find their way to my hair, slipping through the strands at the nape of my neck. He pushes them up until he reaches my bun, curls them into a fist and tugs hard.

"You been listening to your dirty stories again?" *Oh my god. So possessive. So hot.*

"No."

"Making up some filthy fantasy?"

"Maybe," I laugh softly, grinding back, desperately seeking more of his hard length.

Rennie tightens his grip. "Tell me."

"I was thinking about you."

"What about me?"

"This. You. Your fingers."

"These fingers?" He slips two inside me with ease and I clench around them, thick and firm. I don't know whether to focus on the way he slowly strokes inside me, or the sensation of his tongue sweeping up my neck to that sensitive, heavenly spot behind my ear.

He slips his knee between mine, opening me up further. His fingers push deeper until he's cupping me so tightly that his palm rubs against my clit.

"How are you so good at this?" I say, my hips rolling.

"Because I know you."

He hooks my leg over his and rolls me onto my back. Letting go of my hair, he stretches his arm underneath me, reaching down to tug my shirt up. Finding my nipple, he rolls it between his fingers and when he pinches firmly, everything inside me tightens. I didn't know I liked that so much. I turn my head towards his and find him in his own state of bliss. His eyes are closed, he looks relaxed and sleepy as his fingers keep up their slow, delicious exploration. This is a different Rennie to the one who carried me to bed on Sunday night. That Rennie took control of my body and drove me to orgasm full-throttle. This one is unhurried, on a leisurely quest for pleasure. I could let him touch me like this for hours, but the fire within me is building fast.

"Rennie..." I stroke his cheek with my thumb.

"Mmm?" When he opens his eyes, they lock onto mine. I feel a dull ache, a longing for him that comes from deep within. I've felt it before. In the woods twelve summers ago. Under mistletoe at the Thatch Cross Jingle Jamboree. When he held my face after pulling me from the wreck of my car. It's a need for him to see me, to see me more deeply than anyone else does.

"You haven't kissed me," I whisper.

His eyebrows dance up in surprise, a little moan from the back of his throat. "Do you want me to kiss you?"

"Of course. I mean, only if you want to—"

He cuts me off, crashing his mouth to mine. All I can do is moan against his warm lips, and mine tingle when he moans back. I gasp in shock, awe, bliss, and he opens too, his tongue finding its way to mine. Sweeping and exploring. Tasting and devouring. My hands find their way into his hair and I pull him even closer. It's impossible to tell who is kissing who here. I tell him without words how much I need this, and he tells me right back.

This is not a kiss between friends. This is more. The only way I can describe it is that it feels like home.

Beneath the covers, my legs squeeze around his hand, but he withdraws his fingers and pushes them apart again. I ache at the loss of his touch, but not for long. His fingertips find my clit and he strikes up those firm, lazy circles that drove me wild the other night.

I'm already so close, hanging by a thread after a night spent in my filthy brain. Rennie with his hand in my underwear and his tongue in my mouth is almost too much to bear.

He breaks the kiss I never wanted to end, then pulls back a little and stares into my eyes. "Go baby, come."

I grip his arm, that big, firm bicep, with both hands. My fingers barely meet, and I cling on for dear life as white heat ripples through me. My hips buck against his hand, that tight band in my core stretching and stretching until it snaps, sending my orgasm spiraling through me. Rennie doesn't let up. His circles grow firmer, faster, tighter, and I'm completely helpless to do anything but shake and choke out his name as my first orgasm slams straight into another.

I guess we are still doing this then, and that's absolutely fine by me. I can't think of a better way to spend this period of confinement than hopping into bed with him every chance I get. Rennie still hasn't let me touch him, though. After he fell asleep, I dozed with him for a while before getting up. I've been watching TV in the living room ever since, fretting about whether or not to give him this list.

This is insane, right? Actually insane. Part of me is terrified to let him know what goes on in my mind. I've read so much smut over the years that my benchmark for 'normal' is highly skewed. The other part of me is fucking delighted. The way that he's been with me so far, that's exactly what I've been craving. Maybe this list is a way to finally get a little bit more of what I want. He's a horny guy, I'm a horny gal, what have we got to lose? Oh yeah, 30 plus years of friendship, that's all.

He's going to leave soon, and if I don't do it now, I'll lose every ounce of courage I have.

"I left something on the kitchen counter for you," I blurt out as he laces up his boots for his second night shift. He crosses the room and picks up the folded paper.

"Is this a love letter?" he laughs, opening it up.

"If you're hoping for romance, you'll be disappointed."

I watch him closely as he starts to read, and though his expressions remain stoic, his grip tightens like he's holding a winning lottery ticket. It's not long until his eyes widen and I can't stop smirking.

"Jesus Bec," he drags his hands over his face and groans heavily. I wonder which part it was that broke him. The spanking? Maybe the blindfolded edging? Probably the fucking in the woods thing. Fortunately, I left out the bit about doing it in a wedding dress. I haven't completely lost my mind.

"You said you wanted to hear it."

"I did." He folds it up quickly and shoves it in the inside pocket of his coat. "I do, but I can't read this right now though unless I want to die from a boner in the next 12 hours."

"Well. It's yours to do with as you wish."

He's truly speechless, and I love that I have that effect on him. But at the same time, when he doesn't speak to me, that's when I feel most vulnerable. I need to know what's going on in his head, but Rennie has never been one for talking about his feelings.

"Hey Renn," I call after him. "Just so you know. I've never told anyone this stuff before. I trust you."

18

Rennie

No decent firefighter would ever wish for a busy shift, but this one is painfully slow and I need distractions to keep my mind busy and off Bec. I kill a few hours on vehicle maintenance, then review our public safety demonstration materials before our next event. I take on extra cleaning duties, rattling through our monthly deep clean checklist before heading to the gym.

The gym is where I channel my frustration. I have a strict routine. An hour on the treadmill, then three sets of weights. I like the methodical, controlled nature of it. Counting up reps, counting down minutes. It keeps my head straight, stops me spiralling. Fills a physical, animal need to blow off steam.

Bec's list is, excuse the expression, burning a hole in my pocket. I couldn't risk leaving it in my coat, so it's zipped into my shorts. If anyone wants to know her deepest, darkest, dirtiest desires, they'll have to come through me.

This goddamn list. Places, positions, specifics. *Real* specifics. She wants me to pull her hair. She wants me to cover her in lovebites. She wants me to pin her down, throw her around, fuck her in my car, pick her up in a bar as if I haven't known her my entire life. She wants me to call her a good girl *and* a filthy whore.

I don't even know why I told her that was a specific fantasy of mine, except that in that moment the idea of her giving me a list of her desires topped every other scenario I've pictured us in.

All these things I've told myself for years that I can't have, shouldn't even be *thinking* about. Not only does she want them, but she's never told anyone but me. That's what she said. *"And I trust you."* It feels like a trick.

Her handwriting is a little scribbly towards the end, and it occurs to me that I've fucked up, big time. What on earth possessed me to ask her to write me a list when she's still recovering from her wrist injury? It must have taken her ages. This is what happens when I only think about myself. People get hurt.

In a world where I do my best to keep everything under control, the one thing I have no control over is Bec. Didn't plan for her getting injured, didn't plan for her needing to stay with me. Absolutely didn't plan on discovering that she's a horny little maniac who apparently gets herself off multiple times a day thinking about me. Never in a million *years* thought I'd be in possession of a dirty little wishlist that I've promised to fulfil

And I definitely didn't plan for her asking me to kiss her. Sure, I've thought about it a million times, but never thought I'd get another chance after blowing it the first time. We kissed once, you see, years ago, and it was so awful for her that we never spoke of it again.

It was the summer we turned 18, the day we got our A-level result. For months, there'd been a plan to continue the long-standing Thatch Cross tradition of heading into Burrow Woods for a party. Even now I have to scope it out every year, swing by to make sure nobody's lit a fire. I always recognise a few kids from self-defence class, give them my congrats, and then I leave them to get on with it.

Someone had brought some vodka that year. It wasn't as if we never drank, but I dropped the ball and didn't keep a proper eye on Bec. I had no idea how much she'd had to drink.

At some point in the evening, she'd called me over to sit with her on an old tree trunk. It had been there as long as I could remember. Even though we weren't so close anymore, we'd climbed it together hundreds of times as kids.

With the party raging behind us, Bec asked me about my plans for summer; she'd be working in the shop, I'd be starting my firefighter training in a couple of weeks. She'd asked about my dreams for the rest of my life, and in that moment something unspoken passed between us. Her lips found their way to mine, and that was the future I saw.

It can't have lasted more than thirty seconds, but she'd shifted effortlessly into my lap, our hands found each others, tongues met in the darkness. And then she pulled away, hiccupped, and puked all over her shoes.

I felt awful. If I'd known how drunk she was, I would never have kissed her. I was raised better than to take advantage of a woman. You never touch a woman who's intoxicated, never put your hands on them in anger, never take what you want without their consent. I knew it then and I sure as hell know it now.

That night, I left immediately and asked her neighbour, Jamie, to take her straight home. The following morning, I stepped out of my house to go over and apologise, just in time to see her hug him goodbye on her front porch.

I've thought about that kiss a lot over the years, but our kiss this morning, that was something else. All the things I've never said sitting just beneath the surface. Things I'm dying to tell her, if only I could keep my hands to myself for five fucking minutes.

19

Bec

While I'd love a repeat of yesterday morning, I also wanted to shower before Rennie got home from work. Just in case he felt like getting started on my list right away.

I knew getting clean would be a mission, but my heart melted a little when I discovered he had put a stool in the shower for me. Yes, it made me feel 85 years old, but it turns out sitting down to shower is a total game changer. I could wash my hair, I even managed to shave my legs and check out my bruises without falling. Sitting under that hot water with nothing to do but relax? Utter heaven.

When Rennie rolls in, I'm eating cereal at the breakfast bar, gently flexing my ankle one way, then the other.

He looks exhausted, dishevelled, and sad. I want to hug him, stroke my fingers through his still damp hair, but he busies himself rinsing his water bottle and doesn't even turn to look at me.

"Are you going to sleep?" I ask as he makes for the hallway.

"Just a quick snooze. I have Rhyme Time at 11."

"Can I come with you?"

"No."

"Please, Rennie?"

"Hanging out with thirty toddlers is the opposite of resting."

"I can't spend another day watching TV and eating crisps. I mean, I could, but I'm feeling better. I want some fresh air, and I need to check on the shop. Just let me come into town for a bit."

"Fine," he concedes. "Be ready at 10:30."

I'm thrilled to be heading out, excited to see the big wide world. I miss my lovely little town and all those who bask in her glory. And I'm especially happy that I got my way with Rennie, even if he's clearly in a grump about me being out at all. Only once we're on the road into town does he break his silence.

"Siri, call Charlton's Cheeses," he says, and his phone follows his orders. That reminds me, I still need to set these voice activation things up on my phone, should, god forbid, I ever find myself in the unfortunate position of losing my phone in a car crash again. Wait...did he say Charlton's Cheeses?

"What are you doing?"

The phone rings twice before the call connects. "Charlton's Cheeses, Alyssa speaking."

"What. Are. You. Doing?" I mouth and Rennie continues to ignore me.

"Hi Aly, it's Alistair."

"Oh hey, how's my girl doing?"

"She's good. I've got her in the car with me just now. Listen, I'm coming into town for Rhyme Time and I'm gonna drop Bec with you for a bit. Think she's getting a bit sick of being cooped up with me."

Alyssa snorts from the other end of the line. "Yeah right." *That cheeky cow.*

"Can you make sure there's a chair or something for her to sit on? I don't want her doing shit. She's supposed to be resting, but she's terrible at following orders."

"Ha!" she hoots, "I can try."

"We'll be there in five." He ends the call and, though he keeps his eyes on the road, I can see him smiling like he's won this round.

"Rennie, you're not the boss of me," I huff.

"I fucking am, Bec," he says, his voice low and growly. "You'll do exactly as you're told today, and if you don't, there will be consequences. Do you understand me?"

Hooooooly shit.

In the shop, Alyssa has brought the little desk chair down from my flat and positioned it by the rear door for me to sit on.

"This is obstructing a fire exit," Rennie says, picking the chair up like it's made of air. "Come on Aly, you know better than this."

"Sorry, there's not exactly room for furniture in here." He looks around and realises she's right, there's nowhere else for a chair to go. He puts it back where it started.

"How about I just stand? I'm perfectly capable."

"You sit," he says, pointing at the chair until I do as I'm told.

"Yes, Sir," I say like a cocky little shit. I'm pretty sure I hear him curse under his breath and that's how I know I'm getting to him.

"I'll be back in 45 minutes. If there's a fire, you call 999 and get everyone out through the front door as quickly as possible."

"There won't be a—"

"Don't you dare say it!" he shouts, and Alyssa and I both snap our mouths shut.

"And Rebecca," he says, half out of the door. "If I come back and find you up that stepladder, you'll be in a world of trouble. Behave." He winks as he goes and my cheeks burn. *Fucking hell, I love bossy Rennie.*

"Jeez, I want to be in a world of trouble with Rennie," Alyssa says, "That was hot."

I just smile and bite my tongue.

"What's going on with you two?"

Shall I tell her? Can I? Fuck it, I've got to tell someone, this is eating me alive.

"If you speak a word of this to anyone else, I'll fire you as both my friend and colleague."

"Of course," she nods frantically.

"I mean it. You'll never work in cheese again."

"Cross my heart," she says, adding the gesture over her chest for good measure.

"We hooked up."

"*What?*"

"Well, sort of, I mean, I'm pretty useless at the moment," I point to my wrist, still ensconced in this awful wrist guard at Rennie's insistence. "But the other night I told him I was feeling frustrated, you know, sexually, and then—"

"And then *what*?"

"And then he made me come."

"Jesus christ," she bites her fist. "I need details, babe."

"Hand stuff and mouth stuff."

"*Jesus. Fucking. Christ.*"

"I know! I can barely breathe."

"Was he good?"

"Don't ask stupid questions, Alyssa."

"I can't believe it. This calls for champagne." She dashes around, looking for a bottle. "Oh shit, can you drink right now? Are you on painkillers?"

"I can, but you can't. It's 11am and you're running my shop, remember?"

"Oh shit, yes. Sorry, boss." She stares at me and shakes her head slowly in disbelief until we both collapse in a fit of giggles.

An hour later and Rennie is back looking as hot as ever. Unfortunately, he also looks livid, as I'm on my feet behind my counter, apron on, back where I belong.

"What the hell do you think you are doing?" *Oops.*

"How were the kids?" I ask, avoiding his furious glare.

"They were good. Sit down. Now."

I prance over to the chair, making a show of just how capable I am, and Alyssa comes through from the kitchen out back.

"Alyssa, you and I are about to fall out," he says, eyes locked on mine. "You had one job."

"Telling this one to keep still? Yeah, I'm not qualified, sorry," she smirks at me behind his back.

The bell above the door jingles and I lean past Rennie's frame to see Shauna Leary coming into the shop. She looks around, her gaze eventually landing on Rennie's back.

"Oh hi Alistair, I didn't know you'd be in here," she says, placing her hand on his bicep ever so casually. *Yeah right.*

Shauna only comes in at Christmas for a wedge of Stilton and a Lancashire Bomb. She's clearly followed him in. I cross my arms and press my lips together to watch the scene unfold. On she goes with the bicep stroking. *Shameless, absolutely shameless.* "I haven't seen you around much lately."

"I've been busy looking after this one," he says, stepping out of her reach and over to my side. He places one hand on my shoulder, and I feel the heat of his touch scorching through my jumper. It's possessive, yet strangely shocking. Rennie has never touched me in public before. "She was in a pretty bad car accident last week."

"Oh, you're such a sweetheart," she says, never taking her eyes off of him. He could be talking about a cat for all she cares. I don't expect Rennie to tell her exactly how well he's been looking after me, but I wonder what's going through his head right now. I look at the floor, afraid I'll laugh and give the game away.

"I'm glad I ran into you," Shauna fawns. "I was thinking you must come to dinner sometime. My ex-husband has the kids on weekends, so I'm all by myself."

I look from her to Alyssa, just as Alyssa looks back at me, wide-eyed with *WTF* written all over her face. Shauna's ex left her a few years ago, not long after they moved here. I do feel for her, it can't be easy to date with young kids after uprooting your entire life, but she's wasting her time here.

"Yeah, maybe," Rennie says and my heart leaps into my throat. His warmth disappears when he shoves his hands in his pockets and stares at the floor.

"OK, well, you have my number. You give me a call any time you like."

"Will do," he says. *Excuse me? Will do what now?*

Shauna turns and leaves without acknowledging me or Alyssa. She's clearly not remotely interested in keeping up the pretense that she came in as a paying customer.

The door clicks closed, and I burst out laughing. I don't know whether it's shock or anger, but it's unstoppable. Rennie snaps his gaze back down to me.

"What's funny?"

"Rennie, you cannot tell me you don't see that?"

"See what?" he shrugs.

I jab my finger towards the door. "How women are desperate to hook up with you."

"Don't be ridiculous." He turns to Alyssa. "Could I have a piece of the aged gouda, please?" She raises her eyebrows, then lifts the cheese from inside the counter.

He's nuts if he thinks he can shut me down that easily. "You don't have to say, *"yeah, maybe"* you know? You can just say you're not interested. Don't lead her along."

"I'm not leading anyone along. I'm just being polite. Are you jealous?"

"No," I scoff and pick at the velcro on my wrist guard. "Now who's being ridiculous?"

"Okaaaay," Alyssa interjects. She sets Rennie's cheese by the till and points her thumb over her shoulder. "I'm gonna go check stock levels out back." *Real subtle, thanks mate.*

She disappears through to the beaded curtain my Gramps hung before I was even born, leaving Rennie and I in a stare off.

"What do you need gouda for?" I eventually say.

"It's your favourite." *Ugh, how dare he use cheese to be so sweet to me.* "Listen, do you need me to grab anything from upstairs before we go?"

"No, I don't think so."

"Any fresh clothes? More underwear, or... anything like that." Rennie steps closer to me, hands on his hips, head cocked. His eyes blink away as if I know morse code or something. I shrug, then Rennie leans in real close, cups my face, brings his warm mouth to my ear and whispers.

"Do you want me to pick up your vibrator so I can fuck you with it later?"

Ohhh holy hell. Clever man. Filthy man. All is forgiven.

"OK," I nod and press my thighs together. "Maybe a few extra things."

20

Rennie

I park on the street outside Dad's garage. Or my brother's garage, I should say. While I followed in our uncle's footsteps, Jack followed in Dad's and took over the family business. When his days aren't full with services and repairs for everyone in town, he restores classic cars for customers with more money than sense.

I dropped Bec at home on the way here, convinced her it wasn't safe to stand and there was nowhere to sit. Truthfully, I just don't want her to be here for this. Her toys were a welcome distraction on the drive, I enjoy the weight of them in my pocket. I could have left them with her, but the thought of her getting off without me is too much. Maybe I'll surprise her with it later. I like the idea of that.

Inside I find my brother with his head under the bonnet of a Range Rover, fiddling with god knows what.

"How's the wife?" Jack laughs. He sets down his tools and wipes his hands on an oily rag.

"What are you talking about?"

"Heard you shacked up with Rebecca Charlton. Figured if things were moving that fast you might be married by now. You knocked her up yet?"

"I have not *shacked up* with Bec, she's staying with me while she recovers from her accident. An accident that almost killed her, I might add. Show some fucking respect."

"I'm just messing with you, bro. I'm glad she's got someone looking out for her."

A grunt is all he's getting. Though he's a couple of years younger than me, Jack's always had a knack for winding me up. I'm not taking the bait today.

"Where's her car?" I ask, looking around the garage.

"Not here," he says.

"Why not?"

"Never came in."

"Why not?" I repeat. I'm getting more pissed off by the second.

"You know insurance companies only send me easy repairs. Hers must be in a pretty bad way."

"It is. I need you to fix it." I push past him and through to the back room that doubles up as an office and a kitchen. We've made a lot of memories in this little wood panelled space. Me and Jack messing about with toy cars, pissing Dad off with our play fighting. When we were a bit older and Dad let us get to work on fixing a car of our own, we'd be here late nights and all weekend tinkering away.

A framed, yellowing photo of us and Dad still hangs on the wall, one of us on each shoulder under the old Rennie's Motors sign.

Jack comes in behind me and flicks the kettle on. I hover, not feeling dickish enough to sit in the chair behind his desk. Dad always made it clear that the boss and the boss only got that spot.

"How bad is it?" he asks.

"Roof is crushed, doors are all bent out of shape. Needs new windows. Engine might be OK though, I'm not sure."

"Jesus Ali. I'm a mechanic, not a miracle worker."

"That car is everything to her, Jack. You should have seen her in the hospital, it was the first thing she asked about. I need to fix this for her."

"I don't know if I can even get parts that old. Some things can't be fixed, mate. Sometimes you just need to get a new car and move on."

"That's not fucking good enough," I snap.

Jack sighs, but he knows better than to argue with me. "Where is it now?"

"I don't fucking know," I shout. "I thought it was here."

"Listen, you may be the bigger and uglier brother, but stop taking your shit out on me. I'm trying to help you."

Jack returns to his work while I get on the phone to the fire station, then the scrap yard, and finally her insurer. I clean the office windows while I navigate their stupid automated system and when I finally get through to a real person he refuses to speak to me because I'm *"not the owner of the vehicle in question"*. I call him a useless prick and stab at my phone to hang up.

Behind me, Jack throws his tools on the workbench. "Seriously, Ali, what's going on with you?"

"Bec. Bec's what's going on with me," I yell, my last nerve shredded. "I'm trying to sort all this crap out and look after her and—" I can't tell him this stuff. Can't tell him she's all I think about. Can't tell him she's under my skin, and in my bed, and I'm taking way too many liberties with her when she's in no position to argue. I'm supposed to be helping her, for God's sake, not putting my hands on her every chance I get. And no, the knowledge that she wants it too does not make any of this any easier. It's like everything I thought I knew is unravelling before my eyes.

"I just want her car sorted, and for her to be OK." I crouch down and put my head in my hands before I punch a hole in the wall.

"You want to know what I think?"

"No," I grunt.

"I think you've had a thing for her your whole fucking life. I think you'd see she's got a thing for you too if you opened your eyes. I think this accident scared the shit out of you, and I think you're afraid to admit it. I get it. I'd be a mess if something like that happened to Hannah."

Unlike me, Jack manages to not be a total fuck-up when it comes to relationships. He and his wife, Hannah, just celebrated their eighth anniversary. I guess that's more experience than me. And apparently now makes him some sort of guru.

It seems ridiculous now, but I thought I was heading that way with Sophie because that's what people do around here. My parents were high school sweethearts, so were Bec's. When I scared her out of the country, I figured I'd had my shot and blown it.

I sigh and shake my head. "She's too good for me, Jack."

"Bullshit. I don't know why you think that. You're a good man." I look up at him, leaning against the doorframe marked with our heights over the years. I've always been bigger, in age and stature, but from here he's the real deal. A proper grown-up. His face is sincere, he actually means it, and he cares. But he's got no fucking idea what I'm like.

"You've got to tell her how you feel," he says.

I stand up, grab my phone, and push past him. "I've got to go."

"Ali," he calls after me. "Find me the car and I'll see what I can do."

21

Rennie

I swing by the supermarket on the way home and text Bec to ask if she needs anything. Her reply is three aubergine emojis, so god only knows what dinner will be. From the car, I call Bec's folks to give them an update on her progress. Then I try her insurance company again, hoping another person might be more understanding. I just want to give her a bit of good news. If anyone can get her car back in order, it's my brother. I'd feel better if it was under our roof and not rusting in some junk yard somewhere. Once again, it's a dead end.

The house is quiet when I get in. I find Bec dozing under a blanket on my sofa. The low autumn sun streams in through the patio doors, bathing her in gold. It makes my heart ache to see her there. How good she looks. How right it feels to come home to her. I want more of this. To come home to her every day. To cook for her, care for her, be with her.

My uncle isn't wrong.

My brother isn't wrong.

I love Bec, and I have no idea what to do about it. I've never felt like this. I don't have words to describe it, let alone tell her that, for me, this is more than just helping her out.

But the things I crave are not the acts of a man in love. A man in love is caring and gentle. The last time I pushed past that, she moved to fucking Australia. Bec says she's never told anyone about these things she wants, which makes me think she's got no idea what she's letting herself in for.

I try to keep the noise down while I unpack the food, but soon spot her stretching her body out. I see her entire thought process unfold as she takes a second to remember where she is, then turns her head to look for me.

"You're back," she says. A sleepy smile spreads across her face. She's cute as fuck, twitching her nose and rubbing her eyes.

"I'm back." She pulls herself up and while she fixes her hair, I notice something is different. "Why is your wrist guard off?"

"It's fine, Rennie, honestly," she flexes and rotates it. "See. And it was starting to stink."

"Well, take it easy. And get that leg propped up."

"Yes, Sir," she teases and does as she's told.

"How do you want me to cook these aubergines?" I ask from the other side of the kitchen counter.

"What aubergines?"

"These aubergines," I wave one. "You asked for three."

Bec bursts out laughing. I don't get it. "You don't know about aubergines?"

"No, I'm a meat and potatoes guy."

"And here you told me you weren't vanilla," she says, her beautiful, beaming smile plastered across her face.

"Do I need to come over there and show you exactly how not vanilla I am?"

"Oh yes, please." Her eyes light up and she sits up and stretches a little more. I round the kitchen counter but am rudely interrupted by her phone buzzing on the coffee table.

"Ugh sorry, one second." She accepts the call and relaxes back against the sofa cushions.

"How are you doing, my darling?" I hear her mum's voice through the speaker and I hover out of the sight line of her screen.

"I'm fine Mum, honestly. You need to stop worrying."

"That's not what Alistair said." She scowls at me across the room, pointing two fingers back and forth between us. I stalk my way towards her and she tilts her head down to avoid looking at me. When my shins bump her knees she parts them and lets me step closer, just like I'd hoped she would.

"It's just bumps and bruises," she says, eyes on her Mum, still ignoring me. "He's overreacting and won't let me do anything. He's got me locked up here like some sort of—" Bec presses her lips together and stifles a laugh.

"Some sort of what, dear?" Louise says, "I can't hear you."

I step my feet apart, nudging her legs wider. A whimper escapes her throat. I fucking love how hard she's trying to ignore me. I reach down and stroke the back of my fingers along the inside of her thigh.

"Weird signal. I'm fine though, I'll talk to you later Mum!" she hangs up the phone and throws it to the other end of the sofa.

She sits upright, tilting her head back to finally look at me. *Jesus, I can't get enough of her.* That perfect pink mouth, her flushed cheeks. I shove my hands in her hair, just like I always dream of, and tighten my grip at the back of her head. Leaning down, I pause with my face just inches from hers.

"Got you locked up like some sort of what, Rebecca?"

"I was going to say some sort of sex slave, but decided against it."

"Hmmm, were you now? I don't recall seeing that on your list."

Her eyes widen. "You read it?"

"That list is unbelievable. You would really let me tie you up?"

She nods and, as much as it pains me, I let go of her hair and take a step back. "I can't do any of these things with you, sweetheart."

"Oh. Oh god. It was too much, wasn't it?" she squeezes her eyes shut. "OK, please could you kill me now. Pretend this never happened."

"No, Bec, that's not what I mean. I can't do these things with you, right now."

"You have to go out?"

"No. I mean while you're injured."

"I'm not even that bad! I can walk more now. My wrist is fine." She waves it around to prove her point and I reach out to grab it, pull her hand to my mouth, and press a kiss to the inside of her wrist.

"I don't want to hurt you." I nuzzle my face against her palm.

"You won't," she whispers.

I close my eyes and kiss more, but pull away with a low groan when she hooks the fingertips of her other hand into the waistband of my trousers. I'm half erect already just from being in the same room as her. This is unbearable.

"Rebecca..." my voice is low, a warning.

"Rennie..." she mirrors my tone. "I didn't injure my mouth, you know."

Her fingers stroke beneath the elastic, inching down towards my fly, and I thicken with every button she slips free. When she tugs my trousers down to my knees, all I want to do is take my dick out and cram it into her mouth.

Why can't I just want normal things with this woman?

The room goes blurry and I take my hands off her. "Baby, you can't." I swear, if she puts her mouth anywhere near my dick I'm gonna lose my mind. In my head I've already overstepped a thousand times, probably more. I'm holding on by a thread here.

"I can and I will. Please, Rennie? I want to so much." There's surely not a man on the planet who could resist the siren call of her begging.

She keeps her eyes on me, waiting for the barely imperceptible nod I've got no control over. Then Bec, my sweet Rebecca Charlton, drops to her knees and takes my underwear with her.

22

Rennie

"Holy fuck," Bec says when my dick bobs free just inches from her face. I'm hard, heavy, and aching for her.

She has no idea how turned on I've been since she came to stay. Keeping my dick out of the picture when I've been making her come has been a unique brand of torture. I've been stroking myself off to the memory of her orgasms every time I shower, sometimes twice, but it's no use when I see her like this. My resolve is crumbling faster than I can build it up again.

"This is a bad idea, Bec."

She shakes her head and strokes her fingertips gently up and down my length. Her expression is one of awe, even better than I've imagined.

"Nope. This is a fucking great idea. We can help each other out."

"How exactly is this helping you?" My knees nearly give out when she grips the base of me, and swipes my swollen, aching head over her tongue.

"There are things I want to do with you that I haven't done with anyone before. Have you ever done this?" she asks.

"Had a blow job?" I laugh, awkwardly. "Um, yeah."

Stroking the length of me, she licks a long line up from my balls to the tip, circling the head slowly. "Have you ever really fucked someone's mouth?"

"What?" I choke out. She reaches for my hands, brings them to her hair, then curls her fingers around mine until they each hold a fistful.

"That's what I want. I want you to fuck my mouth."

Bec wraps her lips around me and lowers her head, taking me deeper. *This. Is. Not. Happening.* I groan at the sensation and stroke the back of her head, applying the tiniest amount of pressure. When she pulls back with a pop I let go immediately, afraid it was too much.

"Make me take more."

"Fuck, I don't want to hurt you."

"You aren't. I want this," she says, her hands still teasing me with delicious strokes.

"Are you sure?"

She leans her head back, staring straight up at me. "Yes, I'm sure, I'm so fucking sure. Renn, I'm only gonna say this once, so listen very carefully. You don't need to hold back with me. Everything you want, I want. You want to be rough? Be rough. You want to be in control? Go for it. I'm not fragile, you don't need to check in with me. You gave me what I need, now I want you to take what you need. Understood?"

Through ragged breath, I nod. "Do we need a safe word or something?"

Bec rolls her eyes. *You little brat.* "You know me, Rennie. You know me better than anyone. I trust you. If I'm not into it you'll be able to tell."

"OK." *Fuck, she's really going to let me do this.*

"But just in case," she smirks, "let's make it gorgonzola."

"You are ridiculous."

"And horny. Let's go." She opens her mouth wide, swirling her tongue all over me then closing her lips around me and sucking hard. I let her slide up and down a few times and then meet her descent with a shallow thrust of my own. Her moan vibrates through me when I cup the back of her head, holding her in place. I feel her lapping at the underside of my shaft, coating my dick in hot spit.

I push deeper again and when I reach the back of her throat she gags a little. I hate how much I love that filthy sound. I expect her to pull away, but she shocks me by gripping the back of my thighs and pulling me in deeper. I close my eyes and let her hold me there while I try to stay vertical.

When Bec pulls away again, her breath is fast and shaky.

"More," she pleads. "Give me more."

I thrust again, harder this time. Deeper. "That's a good fucking girl." I watch her eyes flutter and love the way my dick muffles those sweet, sweet moans.

I let her come up for air, but she's insatiable and goes straight back down. Glancing past her head, I see her hips rolling in time with her bobbing her head. Her thighs rub together, desperately seeking some relief. I stroke my thumb across her pink cheek, "Do you want to touch yourself?"

With her mouth full, she can't speak, but she nods and moves to push her hand into her shorts.

"Don't you dare." I bend to grab her arms. Gripping her wrists in one hand, I pull them up high above her head. My dick springs free and she gasps down huge gulps of air. "I want you aching for me. Wet and needy."

"I am, I am, I am."

With my other hand, I tug out her scrunchie and gather the loose hair in my fist, wrapping it like a rope. *Fuck, this is everything I've ever wanted.* I guide her mouth onto my cock again and pull her down hard. No matter how often I've imagined it I never thought I'd be here. Never thought I'd be lucky enough to be thrusting in and out of her hot, wet mouth while she moans and gags and writhes at my feet. I'll never forget the way her cheeks hollow when I pull back out. White heat grows from the base of my spine when I see the trail of drool between my throbbing crown and her perfect tongue. *Holy shit.* I sink in again and watch it drip down her chin.

Fuck. This is too far, I didn't think about how this would end and I'm almost past the point of no return. I thrust a couple more times, then pull her off and cup her jaw in my hand.

"Enough, baby."

"No, no, no," she cries. "Please don't make me stop."

"I can't hold off much longer."

"I don't want you to."

I'm so fucking turned on by her eagerness to please me. I've tried so hard, for *years*, to keep my thoughts about Bec respectful. I try to imagine myself being gentle with her, but in those final seconds before my release it is always this image that flashes before my eyes.

Bec on her knees.

Bec with her tongue out.

Bec sucking me down deep.

Bec whimpering when I grab her hair and hold her in place. Her mouth at my mercy.

"Please, Rennie, please. I need it."

I love her like this. Messy, beautiful, tears in her eyes, breathless. I'm helpless when she pulls her hands free from my grip, and wraps her fingers around the root of me. She squeezes me with firm strokes, taking me for all I'm worth, which is nothing.

Nothing. She's too good for me. Too pure for this, but I'm too far gone. She sucks harder still, her tongue swirls, and I see stars when her other hand reaches for my balls. She strokes and squeezes and sucks and in the end it's her fingernails digging into my backside that push me over the edge. Pulling me closer, she swallows me deep, and the room spins. I fall forward, gripping the back of the sofa, and every muscle tightens when my balls explode. My loud groan fills the room and still she doesn't let up, her lips stretched around me until she takes every last drop.

"Oh god, oh Bec, oh Jesus," I pant. I can't breathe, can't see, can't think straight. "I'm sorry, baby."

She swallows hard and finally releases me. She kisses the tip of my dick, which jerks in gratitude and makes her laugh. Leaning back against the edge of the sofa cushions, she stares up at me, her chest heaving for breath. Then she smiles the most beautiful smile I've ever seen. She looks exhausted, and incredible, and fucking proud of herself.

"I'm so happy," she says. "Thank you." *Thank you?* This goddamn woman drains the life out of me and she's thanking *me*?

I'm at a complete loss for words. I tug up my underwear and kick my trousers aside. Sliding my arms underneath hers, I scoop her up and carry her through to my room. I lay her gently back on the bed and duck into the bathroom for a glass of water. When I return she gulps it down, still catching her breath. I kneel on the floor next to her and run my fingers through her hair.

"I'm so sorry," I whisper. I untangle a few knots from where I've grabbed her. "Are you OK? Did I hurt you?"

"Stop apologising. I'm fine. Better than fine."

I don't believe her. I let my head fall to the covers. Bec rolls to her side and reaches out to thread her fingers through my hair.

"Rennie, talk to me. How are you feeling?"

"Ashamed." I'm loath to admit it, but I am. Ashamed for treating her that way. Ashamed that it's barely scratched the surface of things I want to do to her.

"You have nothing to be ashamed of. I wanted that. So much."

"Why? I just don't understand how it can feel as good for you as it does for me."

"I can't explain it, I just know I loved it." She's quiet for a moment, her breath still slowing back to normal. It matches the rhythm of her fingers stroking out at the base of my neck. How does something so simple feel so incredible?

"I think it's that thing of feeling pleasure and pain mixed together," she continues, "but I know you'd never truly hurt me. And it doesn't feel painful, it feels like a beautiful gift. It makes me feel powerful. In the moment, you're in control, but it's me who gives you that power. Does that make sense?"

"I've never thought of it that way."

"You weren't like this with Sophie or... other partners?" She strokes her hand up and down my back.

"Sophie was..." I don't know how to explain this. I've tried to reconcile it so many times, it never adds up in my head. "We were young, we didn't really talk much, we just hung out, more like friends than boyfriend and girlfriend. It took a long time for us to work up to it, but when we finally slept together, I loved it. I was basically obsessed. I couldn't get enough, and I felt like that's all I wanted to do. But then she broke up with me. It wasn't because she wanted to go travelling, it was all my fault. She couldn't get far enough away from me."

"Oh Rennie, you can't possibly still think that, given how things turned out."

"What do you mean?" I ask.

"Sophie's gay," she says, "Or bi, maybe, I don't know, but she married a woman in Australia. They have two kids. How do you not know this?"

"How do *you* know this?"

"Instagram."

"Are you fucking serious?"

She tugs at my t-shirt. "Come up here. Come lie with me."

I climb up and we lay on our sides facing each other. She strokes my chest and I brush my fingers through her hair, tucking it behind her back, tracing down the dip of her spine. This is a totally different kind of bliss, but one I love just as much as her making me come.

"I can't presume to know how Sophie felt, but there's nothing wrong with enjoying sex, or having a high sex drive. I thought you were a boring, vanilla gentleman, and that you'd never be a match for my filthmongering. But I promise you, everything you like is totally fine, as long as it's with someone who likes it too. I'm sorry that Sophie didn't. Not everyone is compatible, you said that yourself."

"How are you so wise, little miss only ever been with one guy?"

"If you think I've only been with one guy you are deluded."

"What? Who? When?" I frown. "Don't answer that. Doesn't matter, and none of my business."

"I've had some crappy experiences too, you know. Jamie didn't want to do half the stuff I wanted, he'd rather play video games than have sex, and it made me think there was something wrong with me."

"Is that why you split up?" I ask.

"No," she sighs. "We split up because he applied for uni and didn't tell me. We were more like friends too. He kept us a secret from his mum and we dated for *two years*."

"What a prick."

"I overheard her at a party telling someone how she couldn't wait for him to meet a nice girl, and it would get him away from *"that awful girl who follows him around like a puppy"*. She meant me."

"Oh Bec, that's horrible." I pull her closer. "Thank fuck they moved, or I'd be round there now to have a word."

"I know you would," she smiles softly. "But what I wanted to say is that I've read enough romance novels to know there's nothing wrong with me. Or you. You can be rough and gentle. You can take what you need while you give me what I want. You don't have to be in control all the time. I can handle it if you let yourself go."

"You don't know what you're saying to me, baby."

"I don't know what you want that you think is so bad. It's probably more normal than you realise. That's why I said we can help each other figure out what we like."

"I don't want to take advantage of you." I whisper against her forehead.

Bec tips her head back to look up at me. "Does it feel like you are taking advantage of me?"

"No, it feels like I'm worshipping you somehow."

"Hmm," she purrs. "I like the sound of that."

"Being worshipped by me?" She nods her head against my chest, and I scoop her hair up, bunching it in my hand so I can get in close to her neck. Fuck, the way she smells is so good, so *her*. "What other kinks have you been hiding under that apron of yours?"

"Mmm, you should know," her voice goes all breathy "You're the one with the list."

"Yeah, I am." I pull back. "And you're in big trouble for writing that with an injured wrist, missy."

"Oh, please," she drawls, climbing on top of me. Straddling my waist, she lifts her t-shirt clear of her head, revealing those beautiful tits I'm so in love with. "How will I ever seek your forgiveness?"

23

Bec

"What do you think you're doing?" Rennie says.

"Oh, do you need a little while to recover? Because honestly, I think I've waited long enough for this."

"You're still supposed to be resting," he says, his big, warm hands settling on my hips. "You haven't even started physio yet."

"Are you really going to make me wait for the doctor's sign-off? I could turn cartwheels right now."

"Don't you fucking dare, Rebecca."

"Ooh," I pout and push my naked chest out towards him, raking my fingernails down his. "So hot when you use my whole name."

"Sit down, Rebecca." His hands come to my shoulders and press me hard down onto his solid length.

"Ugh, you're doing that on purpose now." I give my hips a little wiggle. "And what shall I call you? Sir? Master? Daddy?" I laugh a little. It's not really my kink, but it might be one of his. I'll do anything for this man. Beautiful, kind, gorgeous Rennie with his sex god body and gentle heart.

"Rennie will suffice."

"But that's what I always call you?"

He sits up, takes my chin between his fingers and thumb, and tilts my face towards him. "Except you've never called me it while you're coming on my dick. Trust me, that's all I want to hear."

He pushes up against me, rocking his hips while he cradles my head and peppers my jaw and neck with soft, sweet kisses. I float my eyes closed and feel the rhythm of his heartbeat, in the fingertips I have wrapped around his wrists, in the pulse of his erection, despite the layers of clothing between us. He tugs one hand free, and I hear him rummaging in his bedside drawer for a condom.

"Let me just—" he lifts me up a little to push his boxers down, and I take the wrapper from him and tear it open.

"Let me. I've always wanted to do this."

He scoots up to sit against the headboard, and I roll it on, giving him a firm squeeze for good measure.

With one foot either side of him I rise up to remove my underwear, and when I kick them to one side he grips my calf in his hand, steadying and possessive. Lowering back to my knees, I guide him into position and groan loudly when my slickness welcomes those first few inches home. He wanted me wet, needy, and aching, well he got his wish. I've never felt this desperate for him. *I'm about to fuck Alistair Rendall. I still can't believe this is happening to me.*

"Can you take it?" he moans into my mouth, his hands full of my hair. I turn my nod into a kiss and rock him a little deeper, inhaling sharply when he pulls me down onto him.

"Oh god," I whimper.

"Do you want to stop?"

"No. I love this. Just give me a second." I stay very, very still, holding his bottom lip between my teeth. Once I've adjusted to the size of him, I push further, taking his final inches. Our groans mingle as we kiss deeply, unhurried. I focus on every sensation. His fingertips caressing the bumps of my spine. My nipples peaked against the solid wall of chest. The fine hair on his belly against the smoothness of mine. How right all of this feels.

My Rennie fantasies have escalated to such obscene levels over the years that I've forgotten what it's like to imagine it like this. Slow, intimate, beautiful.

"You'd better not be doing that whole *"I need to commit this to memory,"* thing again," he says, and I burst out laughing.

"I am, sorry. I just... you feel so good, I just need a second to know it's real."

He flexes inside me. It's a feeling I'd happily spend the rest of my life getting used to. "I promise you it's real, baby, take all the time you need."

"God, you're so big." I rock my hips slowly, my hands digging into the mounds of his shoulders to keep myself steady as I find my rhythm.

"If you keep talking to me like that, I'm not going to last long," he says, his open mouth dragging its way along my jaw. "Jesus, that list Bec, I can't believe *you're* real."

"I'm sorry," I groan, riding harder, loving the slap of my skin hitting his.

"Don't apologise. Do you know what a fucking gift you are?"

"If you keep talking to me like that, I'm not going to last long either. Fuck me like you need to."

One hand fists my hair, and he sucks my lower lip into his mouth, biting down hard. The other hand pinches my nipple at the same time, holding every part of me captive.

"What I need is you." He slides to his back, taking me down with him, and wraps me in his arms. One hand presses my face into his chest, the other arm grips tight around my waist, holding me steady. When he surges up into me over and over, I lose the ability to breathe, to see, to think. I may be on top, but right now I'm completely at his mercy. I love the way he takes from me, but what he needs is exactly what I need too. I sit up, arch my back, and grip his thighs to keep from falling backwards.

"Fuck, Bec, look how deep you're taking me. I should take a picture so you can see how hot you are." *Puh-lease, this man cannot be real.*

"Don't you dare stop. I'm so close."

"Grind on me. Use my dick to make yourself come." *You don't need to tell me twice.* I circle my hips, and he fills his hands with my breasts while I keep grinding against him.

He sits up, wraps both hands around the back of my neck, and pulls my face to his. A hard lick across my mouth feels so depraved it sends me spinning. I want to stay here forever, riding him, tasting him, full of him.

The combination of his thrusts and me grinding against the root of him soon has me seeing stars. He must be able to tell because he pulls back a little, taking either side of my face in his hands. My chest rests against his forearms, and he holds me there while he drives up deeper and deeper, over and over.

"Come on, let me feel you come, baby." His mouth finds my mouth, his air is my air, his sweat is my sweat and finally, *at long fucking last*, I shatter around him.

I barely have a second to recover when Rennie nips at my ear, his voice rough, demanding. "Get on your hands and knees."

My body is made of treacle, but I've never moved so fast in my life. Lining up behind me, he rubs himself between my legs with just the tip, taunting and teasing.

"This perfect fucking peach. I've pictured you like this so many times, and it's even better than I ever imagined." He smooths his hand over one cheek, then squeezes hard, massaging. I hear him take a deep breath. "Oh fuck, Bec, I love seeing my hands on your bare skin. Can I spank you?"

"Yes, god, yes." The words have barely left my mouth when I hear the loud crack, followed by the throbbing heat where his palm met my skin. It should hurt, but it feels so good in the dirtiest way.

"I'm so fucking mad at you. You hid this pussy from me. You hid yourself. I could have been fucking you like this for years." I get another hot, sharp smack for my apparent crimes, then feel him nudge his thick head between my slick folds.

Rennie grabs my hair, pulls my head back, and bends to press his face to mine. "You used me. Now I get to use you." When he growls against my skin, it burns with need. Rennie is an animal. Wild, un-leashed, exactly like I dreamed of.

"Bite down on my pillow before the entire street hears you scream my name." *Oh fuck. Yes. YES.* He pushes my head down as his deep thrust knocks the breath from me. He gives me a second to adjust to his size, and I give myself over to him entirely. Rennie digs his fingertips into my flesh and drags his length out of me, tortuously slowly, before plunging back inside. He does it again, and again, every time hitting new depths.

I twist beneath him, angling my shoulders for a better view of him taking what he needs. He's bent on one knee, the other leg at ninety degrees. He looks possessed, obsessed even. Everything about him is pure, unadulterated, male power.

This is everything I've ever wanted.

When he drives inside me, my tight walls grip around him, and he hisses through his teeth. His eyes never leave mine, silently I will him on and he takes this encouragement, my permission, and sets himself free.

"You're mine. You're fucking mine, Bec." He reaches underneath the pillow and pulls out my vibrator - *when the fuck did he stash that* - then turns it on against my most sensitive spot. I cry out his name beneath a garbled sob, and he pounds faster, deeper, each thrust taking me higher, boosting me to the brink of ecstasy.

He rears back and his hips flex with his deepest thrust yet. This time he doesn't retreat, he stays right there, gripping me hard, still thrusting even though he's buried to the hilt. Pulling me back onto him, he lets himself go and comes with a roar that tips me over the edge again. It's as if his orgasm passes directly into me and I take it all, sparks coursing through every vein until we collapse, shaking, to the mattress beneath us.

The weight of him against me is incredible, only a thin sheen of sweat between us as we recover, resurface, breathless and twitching in a tangle of limbs.

"Well, that's spanking off the list," he pants into my hair. "Are you OK? Am I crushing you?"

"I kind of like it," I love it. I love him. I'm utterly in love with him. "Stay there."

"You're so weird."

"I know, I'm so—"

"Don't you dare say you're sorry," he says, dropping kisses around the base of my neck. "I wouldn't have you any other way."

24

Bec

Rennie hovers by the door in the physiotherapists office, with his arms folded and a face like thunder. I feel fine but he won't let me go back to work until I've had this appointment, though he did agree to bring my laptop over, so I've been able to keep on top of shop admin while I've had my feet up.

He's been in a shitty mood all morning, and I've no idea why. We spent last night doing what we've been doing most nights this past week, eating dinner and taking each other's clothes off, but this morning it's like a dark cloud has settled over him. I don't think I've ever seen him this quiet.

The physio, a handsome young guy with Thor-like blond locks, cups my calf as he holds my foot and gently flexes my ankle in various directions. He's seriously hot. If Rennie and I hadn't spent last night ticking shower sex off my list, I'd probably have the energy to concoct a fantasy or two about this guy.

"Any pain there?"

"Nope."

He flattens his palm against the sole of my foot. "Push against me as hard as you can." I do as he says and give him a gentle shove.

"Oh come on now, you can do better than that. Try and push me over." This time I really go for it and I'm surprisingly pleased when he stumbles backwards, shocking us both into a fit of laughter.

"Woah, easy there super girl. You've done a great job of resting while you recover, Rebecca." Behind me, I hear Rennie puff like a fuming dragon. "I saw the photos from your admission and I can see the swelling has all gone, so I'm happy to give you the all clear. You should take it easy when you start running or exercising again, but I'll send you some exercises that will help you strengthen the muscle."

"Great." I hop down from the bed and slip my shoes back on.

"Are you proud of me, Rennie? I did such a good job resting!" I say, poking him in the side as we get back to the car.

"You want me to drive you home?" That's the most he's said all day.

"Actually, there is somewhere else I'd like you to take me."

"Sure," he says. His voice is sullen, and I know he's not going to like it. I take a deep breath.

"I want to drive up to Fenwick's."

He huffs out a sign and shakes his head. "Fuck no, I don't ever want you up there again."

"I need to go. I need to see where it happened."

"Why?"

"I keep replaying it in my head. In my sleep, it comes back to me."

"I have them too, you know?" he says quietly, staring out of the window. "Nightmares."

"I thought you might." Confusion paints his face when he turns back to face me. "Sometimes you talk in your sleep. Unless it's some other Bec you're dreaming of?"

That raises a small smile, and I take it as a win.

"You really want to go there?" he asks and I nod.

"I'll have to drive there again some day. I don't want to be freaking out every time I go." Reaching across the centre console, I rest my hand on his thigh. He looks down at it and then across to me, still unconvinced. "I'd feel better if you were with me."

"Fine," he says, firing up the engine. *I knew that would do the trick.*

Rennie stays silent the entire drive. Once he parks up in a safe spot, he whacks on his hazard lights before walking around to help me get out. I may not be injured any more, but I know better than to rob the man of his gentlemanly duties.

"We should really have high-vis jackets for this," he says gruffly.

"You mean you don't keep them in your car at all times?" I'm teasing, but I can tell from the dark look on his face that he doesn't appreciate my jokes right now. "Relax, it's broad daylight, and this road isn't busy."

"Those conditions lead to some of the worst accidents. Never be lulled into a false sense of security."

I roll my eyes and push past him. The verge between the road and the trees isn't too narrow, but it's muddy in parts and full of tracks where cars have passed each other. I avoid the worst bits, not keen to roll my ankle any time soon, and keep going a little further along the verge. Even from a distance, it's impossible to miss the massive gap in the treeline where the old oak once stood proud. On the other side of the road, there's a huge dent in the hedgerow that brought my beloved car to a standstill. Though the road has been cleared of debris, there's still a section of the fallen trunk at the side of the road, crudely sawn off at one end.

"For fuck's sake, this is such a hazard," Rennie says, immediately taking photos on his phone. "I'll get onto the council about this."

"I don't think I ever realised how big these trees are," I say, my hands on my hips as I stare up at the towering mass. "No wonder it nearly took me out."

"They're dangerous," he shouts. "I'm going to have them all cut down and make sure this never happens again."

I spin in horror. "You are not? Please don't do that, Rennie. They're beautiful, full of creatures, and they've been here forever. It was a freak storm. You're being ridiculous." He knows full well it would be madness to chop them all down. This is the sort of thing we don't let happen in Thatch Cross.

"OK, fine," he concedes. "I won't, but I still hate them." It's then that I notice his chest heaving, and the scowl he's been sporting all morning looks more painful than angry. I trudge through the damp grass to his side and rub his shoulder.

"Hey, are you OK?"

"I'm fine," he shrugs me off and scuffs at the undergrowth with his boot. "I just... I don't want to be here."

I crouch a little, so he's forced to look at me. "What's wrong?"

He rubs his eyes with the heel of his hand, then pulls me into his arms. "That was the fucking scariest day of my life, Bec. Getting out of the truck, seeing your car like that, I thought I'd lost you."

Oh, God. He's really struggling.

"And you didn't. I'm here. I'm OK." I wrap my arms around his waist and tuck my head under his chin. Pressed against him like this, I can hear his heart racing, his breath shallow. I take his hand and guide him over to the fallen trunk. "Come on, let's sit for a minute."

It takes a couple of attempts for me to hop up, but Rennie has my back, literally, and gives me a helpful boost before joining me.

I steady myself with my hands at either side, and we sit like that for a while. Just watching, listening, thinking. I'm feeling so damn lucky right now. If I'd been a second faster or slower that day, I don't know how things might have been.

"I miss my car," I say. It's not like me to be sentimental, but I do. I have so many memories of me and Gramps in that car. She was his pride and joy and I'd promised I'd always look after her. "I rang the insurance people, they said she's in a junk yard in Barton waiting to be scrapped. They'll pay out, but I'm sad. I never got to say goodbye."

I know I'm being an idiot. It's just a box of metal after all, and I should be thankful she kept me safe for so many years. And thankful for Rennie, Alistair Rendall, the sweet gentleman hero, has pulled through for me big time.

He was right, I don't know how I would have coped if I hadn't moved into his place. The kissing, the sleeping in his bed, the countless orgasms, those are bonuses on top of his unyielding kindness.

"Are you going to move back home?" he says, pulling me out of my thoughts.

I turn to face him. He looks miserable, hunched over and staring at the ground. "Is that what this mood is about?"

He shrugs. "I don't know, maybe."

"I mean, I need to go back to mine at some point. My stuff is there. I've probably got a pile of food rotting in the fridge. The bin needs to be emptied."

"I've handled all of that." He sets his hand down next to mine, close yet too far.

Rennie hasn't been easy to read through all of this. Here I was thinking he was just a decent, kind man, while underneath he was keeping some true feelings at bay. Burying them down while putting everyone else first. He's always wanted what's best for me, always put my needs before his. I've never been bold enough to ask him how he actually feels.

Would he even put himself out there like that? In my heart, I know I don't want this to end, and I hope he doesn't either. I reach for his hand and slip my fingers through his.

"Do you want to keep doing this? With me?"

"Like, a friends with benefits thing?" *Ouch. That's not exactly the response I was hoping for.* We've never discussed what this is, what it could be, but what we've started feels like so much more than friends fooling around. Still, this hardly seems like the time or the place to tell Rennie I'm nuts about him.

"How about we head back to yours, have some dinner, and not worry about putting labels on anything? Would that be OK?"

"That sounds great," he says, hopping down. Standing in front of me, he takes me by the hips and lowers me to the ground, where I find myself in the delicious position of being trapped between his warm body and the log at my back.

"I really care about you, Bec. I always have done." When he lowers his mouth to mine, I forget to worry about where this is going, and get lost right here, in the spot where he saved me.

25

Rennie

I don't know what we're doing or how we got here, but we've lit the match, and while she's here in my arms, the thought of ending this is unbearable. This can't be over already. If a friends with benefits thing is the best I can get, then I'll take it.

I want to stay right here with her, but I'm antsy about being back in this spot, loitering at the side of a road with poor visibility. Putting Bec back in danger is not something I ever want to do.

Back in my car, I take care of her seatbelt, pushing her hands aside even though I know she's perfectly capable of doing it herself, and we take off for home. I'm about to ask what she wants for dinner when my phone rings.

"Hold on, let me just get this." I answer from the button on my steering wheel. "Alistair Rendall speaking."

"Hi Alistair, this is Mitch from Essex Country Fire and Rescue Service. Is now a good time?"

"Hi Mitch, is everything OK?"

"I'm calling about your transfer request." *Transfer request? What transfer request?* In the seat by my side, Bec gasps and snaps her head towards me. "I have the paperwork your Chief Fire Officer sent over, along with a glowing recommendation. We have a position available from next month, so I'm calling to arrange a time for us to meet. When might you be available next week?"

A cold sick feeling rises from my stomach. I'd forgotten all about my outburst in Uncle Jeff's office. Surely he didn't think I was serious? Fuck, I hope this isn't binding.

"Mitch, can I call you back? I'm driving."

"Of course, speak soon."

"You're leaving?" she says when the line goes dead.

"Maybe. Yes? I don't know."

"I don't understand. We just—" her words fall away and she shakes her head in disbelief. Her mouth opens and closes, her hand gesturing back and forth between us.

"Pull the car over," Bec says, but there's nowhere I can safely stop without putting us and anyone else on these narrow winding roads in danger. "Pull the fucking car over," she shouts.

"I can't stop here. Give me a second." I drive on, and as the road widens out I find a spot, swinging the car up to the rusted old gates of a cattle field. I kill the engine and shift in my seat, turning my body towards hers. Bec stares out of the window, her arms folded across her chest, teeth scraping across her thumbnail.

"Bec, baby, say something."

"I think for the first time in my life I am actually speechless. I don't get it. Why would you ask for a transfer?"

"I put in the request the day after your accident."

Her head whips round, and my world crumbles when I see tears in her eyes. "Why?" she chokes out.

"I almost lost you, and it made me realise I can't stay here anymore." Her brow knits together. "I can't stay here and love you and watch you live your life with someone else."

"But there is nobody else," she whispers, wiping her face with her sleeve. Oh fuck, I can't bear to see her cry. This is why I'm no good for her, I'll hurt her even when I'm trying to protect her.

"Someday there will be." I put my hand on her knee, but she jerks it away. It feels like having a knife driven into my chest. "Some guy will move here, he'll be perfect for you, and I won't survive it."

Bec unbuckles her seatbelt, throws the passenger door wide, and climbs out. I try to reach for her but she slams the door in my face, just not quickly enough to stop me hearing her sob.

Hands on the rickety, old gate, she locks her arms and hangs her head in between them, taking long, deep breaths. I don't want to touch her if she doesn't want me to, so I settle for leaning back against the bars, right by her side.

"Bec, please, I can explain—"

"You love me?" she cuts me off.

Oh. That. "Yeah. I love you."

"Since when?"

"Since the second I saw your car under that tree. Maybe for a long time before that, too." Her face crumples. I can't tell if she's happy or sad, or both.

"So you realised you love me, and you decided to leave?"

"Yes."

"Then what have these past few weeks been about?"

"I wanted to help you. Give you what you wanted. I know that's selfish, I—"

"Oh right," she says, throwing her hands up in the air. "Because you're *sooo* kind, and generous. Oh look, there's Alistair Rendall being a hero again, helping the sad lonely woman have a bunch of orgasms because nobody else will?"

"It's not like that—"

"*I* know it's not like that!" She punches me in the chest and I wince. She's stronger than she looks. "You're a terrible liar Rennie, you could never fool me. I know you wanted all this as much as I did." She moves to hit me again, and I catch her fist in my hand. "And I'm not sad and lonely, I've had plenty of opportunities to get with other people, trust me—"

A caveman growl rumbles from deep within me and it makes her snort laughing.

"God, you're so hot when you're jealous. Were you jealous of that physio guy?"

"Maybe," I huff out. "Yes."

"You know why I've been single all these years?" she asks. I shake my head. "I wanted to be with someone like me. And I didn't think that was you, but I secretly *really* hoped it was. You said I was hiding myself from you, but you've been hiding from me too, right?"

I let go of the breath I've been holding onto. Her hands come up to my cheeks and she tilts my head so I can't look anywhere but at her.

"Alistair Rendall, are you afraid of me?"

"Of course not." How could I ever be afraid of her? She's beautiful, smart, outgoing, filthy. It's me I'm afraid of. Me who has no self-control.

"Are you afraid to be with me?"

"Yes," I confess. "What if I fuck this up? What if I hurt you?"

"You won't. Or if you do, you'll figure out a way to fix it. Just like if I hurt you, I'll fix it. You and me are fixers. We're always sorting shit out around here, what's another thing?"

"Your heart and your body aren't exactly on par with Rhyme Time and potholes, baby." That earns me one of her beautiful smiles. The loose strands of hair that frame her face blow gently in the breeze.

She steps away from me, pacing back and forth, hands on hips. The look on her face is one of determination, this is how she has always solved problems. Pacing, thinking out loud.

"We're so fucking stupid, you know that?" she says after a minute. "Why have we never talked about this before?"

"I had you pegged to marry a nice interloper who'd moved here from the city for a slower pace of life."

"I thought you were having boring sex with the tennis mums."

"You are obsessed with those women. I think you're the one who is into them."

"Never! They all avoid dairy, how could we ever be friends?"

I don't know what else to say. She knows it all now. How much I want her, crave her, love her. For a long time there's only the sound of the wind in the trees, and her eyes on mine. I don't know if I can make her happy, give her everything she wants, but I'd rather spend the rest of my life trying than end this, us. It's down to her now.

"Rennie, can you kiss me, please?"

I eat up the space between us, bring my hands to her hair, that beautiful bun that has tormented me for years, and take in all the features of her face. Her bright eyes, the last of her summer freckles, that button nose I've known my whole life.

"Don't make me wait any longer," she whispers and I lower my mouth, tug her in close, and give her everything she wants.

Tipping her head back, she opens for me with a moan and I sweep my tongue across hers. I'm addicted to her mouth, these kisses, I need them like fire needs fuel, oxygen, and heat. If I have to go without them I'll die.

"Oh shit," she says, breaking the kiss way too soon. She pulls back to catch her breath. "I forgot to tell you I love you too."

"What?"

"I love you too. I have for so long, I just thought that you were boring in bed and would never want a filthbag like me."

I give her a playful smack on the ass and she yelps. "You'll pay for such insolence."

She's a filthbag alright, but hearing those three words come from her mouth, I wasn't ready for it, and I need a second for it to sink in.

"You OK?"

"I've just wanted this for so long, I don't believe I'm allowed to have you."

"Rennie, we're not friends with fucking benefits, you idiot. I'm yours." She takes my hands in hers, lifting them to her chest, and settles them right over her heart. "All yours."

Then, with that dirty grin I've come to recognise so well, she lowers one and pushes it between her legs. "Completely yours."

Bec putting my hands on her body, showing me what she wants, is so fucking hot. I'll never get enough of this woman, and now I don't have to. "We need to get home before we commit a public indecency crime."

"Yes, we do," she laughs. "But you need to call your uncle first. Call Mitch. Cancel the transfer. Rip it up. I'm never letting you go."

26

Bec

"What are you doing?"

"Holding my girlfriend's hand," Rennie says, squeezing it extra hard.

"People will talk."

"So let them." We're heading out to lunch. Lunch! An actual outing, but my nerves are getting the better of me. We've been here in this cosy little bubble, safe behind closed doors and prying eyes for so long. I haven't considered how other people might react to the news of us coupling up.

"Do you think they'll be OK with it?"

"With us?" Rennie grips my shoulders, turns me to face him, and tilts my chin upwards. "Babe, it's nobody's business, but I'm pretty sure the whole town will be thrilled. You know how everyone's always trying to set us up."

"Yeah, but not with each other. I'm about to be the enemy of every woman in Thatch Cross for taking you off the market."

"Well, that's their mistake. I was never *on* the market."

He opens the door and gestures for me to go ahead of him, but I can't move my feet. "Are you embarrassed to be seen with me?" he teases.

"No." I just don't want everyone knowing our business. They all know I've been staying here, they won't have to be a member of the Amateur Detectives Association to figure out what we've been up to.

"Then get your gorgeous arse out that door and kiss me all over town so everyone knows you're mine."

"Wait! We should tell our parents first, don't you think?" I say, stalling. "I don't want them to hear it as town gossip."

Rennie pulls his phone from his pocket, swipes open his camera, and snaps a selfie with his lips pressed to my cheek. Leaning against the door frame - *god why is that so hot?* - he narrates as he types out a message.

"Got myself a girlfriend. I think you'll like her. Absolute. Demon. In. Bed."

"Do not say that!" I try to grab his phone, but he's too fast, lifting it high out of my reach.

"I'm just kidding. I'll delete the last bit. Even though it's true."

"Shouldn't you ask my dad for permission or something?" I say, and Rennie bursts out laughing.

"What's so funny?"

He pulls me into his arms, looking down into my eyes. I fall a little bit more in love every time he looks at me this way. "First of all, it's not the 1800s. Second of all, I already have his permission."

"What?"

"Yeah, he told me years ago he wished we were together."

"He did not," I say, shocked. "When?"

"After you and Jamie broke up. I saw him in the pub one night and he told me how heartbroken you were."

"Oh god, *Daaad*," I bury my face in against his chest. "That is so embarrassing. I was *barely* heartbroken."

"Well, he knew you were sad. And he told me that you deserved better than him, which was always true. Then he said he'd always hoped we'd end up together."

"Was he drunk?"

"No, that's the best bit. He'd just arrived. And then my dad said he hoped for the same, and a couple of their friends said they'd bet money on us ending up together."

"What did you say?"

"Nothing. I went home and cried into my pillow," he lets out a little chuckle. "Or had a wank thinking about you. One of those."

"I'm so sorry."

"I'm not. They were right all along."

My phone buzzes in my back pocket and I already know who is calling. I answer and hold it up for us both to see. There's no hiding the smile plastered to my face as Dad comes into focus.

"About bloody time, it's about bloody time," he says.

"You finally did it son, congratulations!" says Andrew, Rennie's dad, squeezing into frame, his big hand slapping my dad on the back. In the background, our mums are screaming, clinging to each other while they jump up and down.

"Mike, get the champagne open!" my mum shouts across the room. "Jan! We're gonna be sisters!"

Rennie and I screw our faces up at each other. "I don't think that's how it works," he says.

"Well, we're bloody thrilled for you kids. We're gonna celebrate all night." There is more screaming from the background. A lot more.

"That's great Mike, thanks Dad," Rennie says, taking the phone from my hand and regaining control of the situation. "We're just heading out for lunch. Can we give you a call later?"

He doesn't wait for a reply before hanging up and tucking my phone back into my pocket.

"See. Everybody's happy. Come on, I'm hungry and I want to take my woman out for lunch before I come home and eat her for dessert."

We take a window seat in Books and Beans, our brilliant bookshop slash coffee shop, and I watch the world go by while Rennie orders at the counter. I have to stare out of the window because I'm too nervous to look around. If someone in here sees us, the rumour mill will be in overdrive. I don't know how he's so comfortable with this.

When he returns with coffees, he takes his seat and reaches across the table to link his fingers with mine. Plopping a sugar lump into my mug, he stirs it for me without letting go of my hand. It's actually disgusting how hot he is. Sitting across from me in a cafe surrounded by books, his hair pushed back, black hoodie fitting him like he belongs on some Beautiful Men Pinterest board. His smug grin says he knows what I look like naked. Which, of course, he does know, very well.

Two palms smack against the window outside, shocking us out of our lusty stares, and I see Mrs Marshall, the head of Thatch Cross town council rushing for the door. Once inside, she pushes past a queue of customers to reach us.

"Rebecca Charlton, my dear, how wonderful to see you back on your feet. We have missed you so much around town. How are you feeling?"

"Much better, thank you," I say, blotting latte foam from the corners of my mouth with my napkin. "And thank you so much for the gift basket."

"Of course, my dear, anything for you." She pats my arm gently while she speaks. "Now listen, there'll be an official invitation coming to you in the mail, but now that I have you, I want to let you know that the town council voted unanimously for you to switch on the Christmas lights this year. Would you do us the honours, dear?"

My mouth hangs open, the room slowing around me as I take in what she's said. "You're not serious?"

"I am a very serious person Rebecca, have you ever known me to joke?" I shake my head. "Our town almost lost you and we'd have been a much worse place if we had. I think it's only proper that we show you how much we appreciate you and everything you do."

I look across to Rennie, his beautiful, beaming face. He knows I've wanted to turn on the Christmas lights since I was a little girl. Since the Christmas they brought in someone from a reality TV show about an airport and they called the town by the wrong name. Our primary school class had been asked to write questions and obviously mine was *"What's your favourite cheese?"*. Gramps and I had stared at each other in horror when the so-called celeb had said "string cheese". I've never gotten over it.

"I'd love to," I say, "I would be so honoured. Thank you so much."

"Well, I'm thrilled, and frankly a little embarrassed we never asked you sooner," she says with a nudge and a wink.

I can't speak, too caught up in the excitement and the vision of me standing on that platform pressing that big red button like I've always dreamed of.

"Well, I won't keep you, but I must say I'm very glad to see this is happening at long last." She waves her hands back and forth between Rennie and I. "Just delightful."

Then she's gone, leaving us to continue eye-fucking each other over the rim of our coffee cups.

"Did everybody know about us, except us?" I ask him.

"I think we knew all along, baby. We just needed a little push."

27

Bec

Six Months Later

On the face of it, nothing has changed at all. Rennie fights fires, entertains toddlers, teaches teenagers how to stick up for themselves, and helps old ladies across the street. I serve cheese and wine and daydream about all the ways I want to take his clothes off. Together we busy ourselves with jobs around the town before the Easter celebrations begin. But at night, everything is different.

Sometimes Rennie stays at mine, sometimes I stay at his, but wherever we are we eat together, we laugh, we play, and Rennie, on my insistence, always sleeps naked. In all my years of fantasising about him, I never had any idea it would be as good as this. When I'm with him I feel completely, truly myself. And when I'm not with him, I'm counting down the minutes until I'm back in his arms.

I left Rennie in bed this morning, begrudgingly I might add, to head up to the Fenwick estate before I open the shop. Alyssa set everything up for a fairytale wedding yesterday, the first of a busy spring season, but it's my turn to collect all our tableware. Even though I've passed that gap in the treeline a few times since the accident, it always makes me hold my breath. I'm not sure why. Partly fear of what could have been, partly gratitude for that old oak that changed my life forever.

I'm heading outside with the last crate of decorations and find Rennie leaning against my van. His arms are folded across his chest and I thank my lucky stars it's mild enough for just a t-shirt. The sight of those biceps straining at the sleeves sends heat straight to my core. *Yum.*

"What are you doing here? Oh god, was there a fire?"

"Only in my loins," he winks. "I'm here because I have a surprise for you." He takes the crate from my arms and carries it for me, dropping it in the side door of the van.

I must say, I loved my old car, but having a work van is an absolute godsend. It has so much space! I don't need to unload everything and store it in my flat at the end of each day, and with our logo and contact information on the side, it's free advertising everywhere I go. Our wedding catering diary is busier than ever.

"Close your eyes, baby," Rennie says, closing the door and turning back to me. Standing behind me, he clasps one hand over my eyes, the other on my hip and nudges me to walk ahead. I step slowly, both of our feet crunching in the gravel, excitement building in my chest. There's nothing here, I have no idea where we're going, or what he's doing. We walk a little and then he turns me, on a little further and then another turn. We're around the side of the building, I think.

"Stop here," he says, releasing me and pressing a kiss to my temple. "You can look now."

I open my eyes and I'm certain I must be dreaming. My car! My Grandpa's beautiful old Ford Cortina, she's here, right in front of me.

"Oh my god, Rennie, you did this?"

"Jack did this. I helped a little, but he gets all the credit."

Tears burst from my eyes, I can't help it, I never thought I'd see her again. "I thought she'd been scrapped."

Rennie steps up behind me, wrapping me in his warm arms. "I know you did. I couldn't let that happen, so I had her picked up. We've been working on her in secret for months."

That's it, I'm gone, full, snotty, uncontrollable sobbing now.

"Shhh, baby, it's OK."

"I know," I shudder, and wipe my face with the back of my hand. "These are happy tears. I'm just so lucky. Lucky to be alive, lucky to have you, lucky, lucky, lucky."

"While we're here, I have another surprise for you."

"Another?" I sniff and regain my composure. "It really is my lucky day."

"Oh, you have no idea, baby. Your ankle feeling OK?"

"It's fine, it's been fine for months." I twirl it around for show, but I nearly lose my balance when he grabs me and yanks me closer. In one quick motion, he spins me to face away from him, pins my arms behind my back, and holds me tight against his chest.

"You see those woods over there?" He nods his head towards the treeline beyond the meadow. *Oh fuck.* That deep, growly voice. I'm in big trouble.

"I'll give you a head start. You can hide, but I'll always find you."

Surely not. Not now.

My heart rate kicks up a gear, my blood wooshes in my ears. Rennie lowers his mouth to my neck and takes a long, possessive, animalistic lick until he reaches my earlobe and tugs it between his teeth. "Run."

28

Epilogue – Bec

Eight Years Later

Archie uses both hands to push through the shop door and, after a minute of checking over the window display, I follow him inside.

"Oh, here comes the tennis mum," Rennie calls out, laughing away behind the counter. I roll my eyes, but I can't help smiling. Despite stepping up into his Uncle Jeff's Chief Fire Officer position when he retired last year, my gorgeous husband still helps out in the shop so I can spend some quality time with our son. Turns out he's quite the tennis champ at just seven years old.

Rennie finds it hilarious that I've become one of the mums I used to be so snobby about, but it turns out they're a pretty great bunch, and I was shocked to discover they do in fact eat dairy. They also drink wine, read romance novels, and have minds almost as filthy as mine. Which is to say, our monthly book club is a riot.

"How'd you play today, buddy?" Rennie asks, ruffling Archie's hair while our boy hugs him round the waist.

"I was great. Won two, drew one." He lets go and starts digging for a packet of crisps from the display basket by the till. A cheeky perk of being the owner's son. He takes two different flavours and tips one into the other, shaking to mix them. Archie gets his appetite from his dad, and his name from my Gramps.

I round the counter and Rennie pulls me into his arms, lifting my chin up for a firm kiss that's full of longing. In the beginning of our relationship I felt super awkward about PDA, a hangover from all the years spent hiding my feelings about him. Rennie, on the other hand, has never gotten bored of showing the world who his girl is. "There's a parcel for you out back," he says with a wink and squeeze of my bum.

"Can you please stop sending sex toys to the shop?" I say through gritted teeth. "Those aren't as discreet as you think." Our local postie knows a lot more about me than either of us is comfortable with.

"Well, I don't want the Boss ripping into them at home," he whispers through his own forced smile, nodding his head towards my feet.

I crouch down and whip back the curtain that conceals the cubby beneath the counter.

"A-ha! I was wondering where you were!"

"Ahhh, Mama! I'm working!" says the red-faced little girl, whose 'work' appears to be unravelling receipt paper. Rennie is not wrong about the parcel thief. At four years old, our daughter, Grace, has zero respect for people's boundaries or personal belongings. I leave her to it and throw on my apron to relieve Rennie. There's no reasoning with her when she's on one of her missions.

A born gossip, Grace fits right into this town. She always wants to know what people are buying, where they've been, and our regular customers joke that she'll be taking over from me before I know it. I think Gramps would absolutely love that.

Rennie as a father has been the most incredible thing to witness. His doting through my pregnancies bordered on unhinged, with him refusing to let me do almost anything from the 6 month mark. But as soon as I saw our babies in his arms, it was all worth it.

"Mama," Grace pipes up from my ankles. "What does this say?"

"What does what say, honey?"

"The words."

I crouch down to see what she's pointing at. I used to love hiding out in this spot when I was her age. In the end I have to lie down to see it and my heart bursts wide open when I realise what I'm looking at. There on the underside of the shelf are the outlines of two small hands, our names scribbled above them.

"Oh my god," I gasp. "It says Rebecca loves Alistair."

"Who's that?" Grace asks, squishing in alongside me.

"That's us honey, that's me and your Dad. Bec is short for Rebecca, and your dad's name is Alistair, but most people call him Rennie, like our last name."

I can't remember how old we were, but it must have been a long summer. Our parents often sent Rennie and me to hang out with Gramps, knowing there wasn't much mischief we could get up to on his watch. Sometimes he'd leave us in charge while he ran errands, and that's when our pent up mischief broke free.

"Rennie!" I call out, "come see this."

"Mama, you're bad! We're not allowed to draw on walls, you said!"

"I know baby, this was very cheeky indeed. Your Dad made me do it."

"You looking at our hands?" I hear Rennie say, and when I look down the length of my body, he's straddling my legs.

"You remember this?" I reach out and he helps pull me up from the floor.

"Of course I remember. You forgot? Oh, you are in so much trouble," he says, pulling me into his arms. I hope I never stop feeling that giddy rush I feel when he holds me tight.

"Why did you do it, Daddy?" Grace says, climbing up his leg until he lifts her into our embrace.

"We used to play a game called Truth or Dare, and I was hoping your mum would choose truth so I could ask her if she loved me. But she said dare," he shakes his head at me, "so I dared her to tell me by writing it on the wall."

"I would never have been so naughty to write on the wall," I explain, tucking Grace's wild curls behind her ears, "so I wrote it down here instead where my Gramps would never see it."

"So Daddy was always your boyfriend?" Archie says, now halfway through a shiny green apple.

"Sort of," I answer, looking up at my beautiful, brilliant, brave man. He is ageing so well. Crinkles around his eyes from years of laughing with me, a dusting of grey hairs around his temples, but still a full head of hair. He's as strong as always, those warm, firm muscles filling out his clothes. I still can't get enough of him. Every anniversary we exchange sexy wishlists, and the butterflies in my stomach kick up just as much now as they did then. "I always had a little crush on him."

"Well, I had a huge crush on her," Rennie says, his eyes full of love. "Still do."

"How old were you?" Archie asks, crouching down to take a look too.

"Like ten," I laugh.

"That's disgusting," he says. "You can't be in love when you're ten."

"I know," I say, reaching out for Rennie's gorgeous face, "but I did love him. Still do, too."

THE END

Bonus Chapter

If you're not ready to say goodbye to Bec and Rennie, enjoy this free bonus chapter that picks up right after Rennie tells Bec to run.

Download your copy at https://BookHip.com/THMMKRX

The Best Book Boyfriend

Who needs real-life love when you have a shelf of perfect Book Boyfriends?

Kara has sworn off men ever since The One dumped her without warning. Instead she spends her evenings reading books with guaranteed happy endings, crushing on fictional heroes who'll never let her down.

Luke is piecing his life back together after the death of his wife. Opening Sunshine Coffee was the first step, but he has no idea where to go from here.

When Kara stops by her new local coffee shop, Luke's clueless comments about the romance novel she's reading are the opposite of a Meet Cute. Determined to make a better impression, he asks for a recommendation to change his mind.

Three books later, he can see the appeal. Who knew reading about fictional people getting laid could teach you so much?

As their friendship blossoms into something more, their painful pasts threaten to keep them apart. But if romance stories have taught them anything, it's that there are many routes to love.

One road trip, a fake date, and a spicy readathon later, can Kara and Luke separate fact from fiction and find their very own Happy Ever After?

Acknowledgements

The inspiration for this novella came to me in the summer of 2022, when I was driving home from officiating a beautiful wedding. I picked up my phone to play my latest audiobook, then immediately panicked. What if there was an accident on the way home, and I had to be rescued by a firefighter and my book was still playing. How mortifying would that be?

I drove home in silence, and by the time I arrived, I knew everything there was to know about Bec and Rennie, their beautiful friendship, and the unfortunate accident that threw them together.

Writing this book has been an absolute joy, and I cannot thank you enough for reading it.

Huge thanks also to Frankie Rose for bringing Bec and Rennie to life with this beautiful cover.

Endless thanks to Katie Sadler, Hayley Dunlop, Amy Richards, Cara Conquest, Katie Khan, Eloise Rickman, Alexandra Muir, Becky Brynolf, Sara Madderson, Gemma Brady, and Nicola Burke for your feedback and encouragement.

Thank you to Gina LB, Holly R, Mary-Jane F, Laura F, Tara E, and Ellie G for letting me gossip about people who aren't even real.

Thank you also to everyone who has ever said *"I can't wait to read this!"* You genuinely kept me writing.

And to Alex, for everything.

Printed in Great Britain
by Amazon